Books by Matt Christopher

Sports Stories

THE LUCKY BASEBALL BAT
BASEBALL PALS
BASKETBALL SPARKPLUG
LITTLE LEFTY
TOUCHDOWN FOR TOMMY
BREAK FOR THE BASKET
BASEBALL FLYHAWK
CATCHER WITH A GLASS ARM
THE COUNTERFEIT TACKLE
MIRACLE AT THE PLATE
THE YEAR MOM WON THE
  PENNANT
THE BASKET COUNTS
CATCH THAT PASS!
SHORTSTOP FROM TOKYO
JACKRABBIT GOALIE
THE FOX STEALS HOME
JOHNNY LONG LEGS
LOOK WHO'S PLAYING FIRST
  BASE
TOUGH TO TACKLE
THE KID WHO ONLY HIT
  HOMERS
FACE-OFF
MYSTERY COACH
ICE MAGIC
NO ARM IN LEFT FIELD
JINX GLOVE
FRONT COURT HEX
THE TEAM THAT STOPPED
  MOVING
GLUE FINGERS
THE PIGEON WITH THE
  TENNIS ELBOW

THE SUBMARINE PITCH
POWER PLAY
FOOTBALL FUGITIVE
JOHNNY NO HIT
SOCCER HALFBACK
DIAMOND CHAMPS
DIRT BIKE RACER
THE DOG THAT CALLED
  THE SIGNALS
THE DOG THAT STOLE
  FOOTBALL PLAYS
DRAG-STRIP RACER
RUN, BILLY, RUN
TIGHT END
THE TWENTY-ONE-MILE
  SWIM
WILD PITCH
DIRT BIKE RUNAWAY
THE GREAT QUARTERBACK
  SWITCH
SUPERCHARGED
  INFIELD
THE HOCKEY MACHINE
RED-HOT HIGHTOPS
THE HIT-AWAY KID
THE DOG THAT PITCHED
  A NO-HITTER

Animal Stories

DESPERATE SEARCH
STRANDED
EARTHQUAKE
DEVIL PONY

Run, Billy, Run

Run, Billy, Run

by Matt Christopher

Little, Brown and Company   *Boston*   *Toronto*

FIRST PAPERBACK EDITION

Library of Congress Cataloging in Publication Data

Christopher, Matthew
  Run, Billy, Run.

  SUMMARY: When 14-year-old Billy joins the track team,
he improves his running and other areas of his life too.
  [I. Running—Fiction]   I. Title.
PZ7.C458Bo   [Fic]   79–20627
ISBN 0–316–13993–9

10 9 8 7 6 5 4 3 2

VB

Published simultaneously in Canada
by Little, Brown & Company (Canada) Limited

PRINTED IN THE UNITED STATES OF AMERICA

to Al and Alice

Run, Billy, Run

Chapter 1

"CAN I HELP YOU?" asked the druggist.

"Yes. I need some medicine for my sister." Billy took a deep breath and tried to stop panting. "She's got a sore throat."

The druggist's shaggy white eyebrows arched. "Coughing, too?"

Billy nodded. "Yes."

The thin-faced man behind the counter looked up over his glasses at Billy, blinked, and went after the medicine. Over his shoulder he tossed another question. "You look beat. Walk all the way from home?"

"No. I ran," answered Billy.

The druggist paused and shot the six-foot-one boy a long, perceptive look. "Ran? That's about two, three miles, isn't it?"

Billy shrugged. "I guess so."

He didn't know how far it was. There was a path workmen had made from the homes beyond the stone quarry all the way to the cement plant across the railroad tracks from the drugstore. It could be two miles or three. But it was an easy run, for part of it was flat, only a little bit of it was up and down because of the quarry, and the remaining part was downhill.

No, running from his house to the little one-horse town called New Court wasn't bad. It was the long haul back that bit like teeth into his calves and thighs. Billy's father had walked it five days a week for three months, and Billy remembered how he had complained about it until he found a fellow workman with a car who would give him a ride. The guy wanted three dollars a week for the accommodation, and his father gave it to him. It was better than walking, he said, especially when it rained. And snowed.

The druggist got the medicine, wrapped it up in white paper, and secured it with tape. "That'll be one sixty-nine, son," he said. He smiled at the boy. "The directions are on the bottle. I'm sure it'll fix your sister up so's she'll be up and around again in a short time."

Billy handed the druggist two one-dollar bills, stuck the bottle into his coat and the change into his coin purse, said good-bye, and started for the door.

"It's raining, son," the druggist reminded him. "Didn't you bring an umbrella?"

"No. I just have this raincoat. I'll be all right."

"Hang around for a while. Maybe it'll clear up soon."

"Can't," said Billy. "My sister's pretty sick."

"If she's too sick, maybe she should see a doctor."

The last words reached Billy just before the heavy glass door closed with a clang behind him. Sure, a doctor, Billy thought. We have to be pretty sick in our house to go to a doctor. He started running immediately, one hand inside a pocket of his raincoat, gripping the bottle, the other held at his side. The rain was coming down hard and steadily, assaulting his head and face, his raincoat, pants, and shoes. The raincoat came only to the middle of his thighs, leaving most of his long legs exposed to the downpour. In just a few minutes his brown hair, which he kept just short enough to leave his ears exposed, was drenched and pasted to his head.

When he had left for the drugstore no one at home could know for sure that it was going to rain. The southwestern sky was darkening up, but in the north and east the shining sun had left the impression that it was going to keep on shining for another three or four hours. It hadn't worked out that way. Now black clouds rolled and swirled. Lightning streaked the sky, pierced the earth like jagged spears. Then came the cannon shots of thunder, and it seemed that with each one another vent burst open and more rain poured.

It was April, usually the rainy month, although it wasn't always so. Because of their location among the many lakes of central New York State local weather prophets said that April was as likely to bring snow as rain. But then again, when they thought back two or three years they remembered an April that had more sunshine than rain or snow. How can you explain that? Billy smothered a rain-smeared smile as the amusing memories of conversations with local characters tumbled through his mind. Nobody could outguess the weather, that's all there was to it. But, as Billy had learned in one of his textbooks, New York's topography and location had a lot to do with its wide variety of climate. Heavy snowfall and extreme changes in the temperature were characteristics of the mountain and plateau regions.

He reached the end of the block, crossed the short bridge that straddled Sawmill Creek, and in another hundred feet arrived at the beginning of the path that snaked up the steep hill that would eventually lead him home.

New Court's population hovered about the six hundred and fifty mark. Most of its homes were built on the hill on the other side of the creek he had just crossed. Its commercial establishments were limited to a post office, a grocery store, a garage-and-gas-station combination, and the drugstore. For anything else that a person needed he would have to drive eight miles to the city of Lonsdale. And if sickness or accident demanded the confines of a hospital, Lonsdale Memorial was four miles farther on.

At this point of his life Billy Chekko hadn't quite decided on where he would like to spend the rest of his life. He just knew that it wasn't going to be in that small, stucco home stuck among the dozen or so similar homes just beyond the stone quarry. But, until that day when his mother and father decided to make a move to someplace else, that's where he, brother Dan, twelve, eleven-year-old Christina, and six-year-old Sheri would stay.

The side of the hill was almost all rock, but a series of odd-shaped, flat-topped shales all the way up made a natural, if uneven, staircase. Billy climbed the steps rapidly, and finally reached the top where the ground leveled off considerably and made running much easier. On both sides of the path weeds grew to shoulder height, and scattered among them were chokecherry trees that hadn't yet started to blossom, skeleton growths of sumac, and an occa-

7

sional elm, pine, or oak, all bending under the lash of the storm.

He began to breathe harder and faster, and felt his heart pumping rapidly, so for a while he walked. He kept his strides long, but not fast. Sometimes the path was so narrow that he brushed against the wet, bending weeds. His pantlegs were soaked and clinging to his legs, and with every step he took he could hear the squish of water inside his shoes.

Billy changed his walk to a run again when he realized he wasn't far from the stone quarry. The quarry was about half a mile wide where he had to cross it, and the stucco houses were about a quarter of a mile beyond it.

It wasn't long before he reached the quarry. It wasn't too deep where the path led across it to the other side, and perhaps only about forty feet deep at its lowest point. But it was broad, covering many acres. Millions of tons of stone had been dynamited and carried out of it to the plant down by the lake to be mixed with other ingredients and processed into warm, soft, powdery cement.

Billy raced over the solid rock floor, running with his knees high, each long stride taking him closer and closer to the other side. Suddenly irritation welled up in him as he saw, not far ahead of him, a small lake.

It was new. It wasn't there when he left home. The rain had done it, formed a lake in just those few minutes that it poured.

"Damn!" he said.

He paused near its edge and looked to his left and right. He was practically in the middle, so neither way would get him to the opposite side quicker.

He remembered a path far to his left that led up to the road going past his home, so he turned and headed for it. He had to skirt potholes, but eventually he found the path, took it, and in a few minutes was up on the hill. He was dead tired now, breathing so hard he had chest pains. His calves felt as if knives were stuck into them. He told himself that the first thing he was going to do when he got home was to rip off his drenched clothes and soak himself in the tub.

He reached the road. It was a macadam, but cracked and seamed from age and the elements.

He figured it was now about a half to three quarters of a mile to his home. The rain had let up a bit. The dark clouds were moving northward, and the booms of thunder were coming from farther away.

He heard a car come up behind him, and got off the road to let it pass.

"Hey, Billy!" a voice yelled as the car pulled up

beside him. "What are you doing out in this rain? Training?"

He grinned, noticing that it was Seattle Williams riding with Cody Jones, who lived in one of the stucco houses. The two guys were pretty good friends, even though Cody was seventeen — just old enough to hold a driver's license because he had completed a high school driver education course — and Seattle was fifteen. Bill couldn't understand why anyone would hang around with Cody. He seemed such a conceited jerk.

"Hop in!" Seattle invited.

Billy, too tired even to talk, headed for the right rear door. But, before he got to it, Cody sped off.

Angered, Billy stared at the car, a green, five-year-old Ford that looked twenty, and muttered, "I love you, too, Cody, you punk."

He started to run again, and saw the car stop about twenty feet ahead, wheels skidding. Billy saw Cody looking back at him through the rear window. He was smiling.

Okay, Cody, Billy thought. I'm in no mood for games. Not in this rain. Not the way I feel. Are you going to give me a ride, or are you going to play around?

Billy almost reached the rear door again when Cody repeated the dirty trick: stepped on the gas and shot the car forward. About twenty feet ahead the car slithered to a stop. This was the third time, and Billy's anger had mounted so that it showed in his narrowed blue eyes.

I'll get you for this, he thought.

But he knew he wouldn't. Cody was shorter, and Billy probably could beat him. But Billy would never fight Cody. He would just be angry about it for a while, then forget it, because the truth was that he had never been in a fist fight with anybody in his whole fourteen years.

Now, when he reached the car, both Cody and Seattle were looking back and laughing at him, as if it were all a big joke.

Sure it is, thought Billy.

He opened the back door, said, "Thanks, buddies. But, no, thanks," and ran on, leaving the door wide open.

He heard the car door slam shut, then the gears grate as Cody shifted it into first, then the loud roar of the motor as Cody stepped hard on the gas and sent the car blasting past him. Water from a puddle in the road splashed up against him, but his pants were so wet anyway that a bit more made no difference.

Billy smiled as the car zipped on ahead. In the few seconds that the back door had been open some rain must have poured into it, wetting the seat. Well, it probably needed a good washing, anyway, he thought with satisfaction.

His home was the fourth one from the end. All the houses on his block looked alike, as if formed out of one mold. Patches in the roofs and gouges on the east sides were grim evidence of falling rocks from the blasting that took place in the quarry once or twice a month.

Billy leaped up on the porch, dropped off his raincoat, barged into the house, and handed his mother the bottle of medicine for Christina. Then he did what he had promised himself to do — get out of his clothes and get into the tub.

It was while he was soaking that he thought of what Seattle Williams had said from the car: "What are you doing out in this rain? Training?"

Seattle and Cody were runners on Cove Hill Central School's track team.

Beginning today, Billy Chekko promised himself, he was going to be one, too.

Chapter 2

THE HOT BATH made Billy feel a hundred percent better. It made him feel clean and even relieved his aches and pains.

After he dried himself with a towel and dressed in dry clothes, he went into Christina's bedroom to see how she felt. With her lovely blond hair cascading over the pillow, and her eyes closed in sleep, she looked more like a china doll than she did a real live girl.

Not wanting to awaken her, he tiptoed out of the room, closed the door, and went to join the rest of the family in the living room. His father was reading the morning paper; Billy's mother was snipping out coupons from the paper's grocery section; and the kids, Dan and Sheri, were sprawled out on the floor, playing Chinese checkers.

"Christina's asleep," Billy said to his mother. "Did you give her any of that medicine?"

"Yes. And I hope it makes her feel better, poor kid. You look much better, too, Billy." His mother's blue eyes looked sadly at him. "I shouldn't have sent you. After that storm hit I worried about you every minute."

"I was okay," said Billy. "Just got wet, that's all."

Dan and Sheri glanced briefly up at him as he found a seat next to his mother on the sofa, then turned their attention back to the game. Billy was surprised to see that Dan was home and so obviously contented with what he was doing. Dan was like a restless colt, always on the go. He was seldom home, even in bad weather. Had the rain *really* kept him in the house?

When Billy asked Dan, Sheri answered. "He was at Joey's. But when it started to rain Joey's mother told him he'd better go home."

"Shut up and play," Dan said.

Billy smiled.

"Shall I fix you a hot chocolate?" his mother asked him.

"Okay. A hot chocolate will hit the spot, Mom, and let's make a cup for your wandering son and his sister over there on the floor."

The bus stopped in front of the house at seven-twenty the next morning. The children were all ready, lunches and books in their hands, waiting for it.

Billy and Sheri sat together. Dan went all the way

to the back to sit with his friends. Christina had a good night's sleep, but wasn't well enough to go to school yet. She probably would make it tomorrow. The medicine had been a definite help.

The bus stopped in front of the Jones's house and both Cody and his younger brother, Al, got on it. As Cody came down the aisle he looked at Billy. His lips parted, and a cold glint came into his eyes.

"See you made it all right, beanpole."

"No problem," said Billy.

He hadn't thought much about Cody because he seldom saw the guy. Being a senior, Cody wasn't in any classes with Billy. They were practically neighbors and Billy had always been prepared to like Cody. It might have been the difference in their ages, but Cody always ignored Billy when he wasn't being mean to him. Why then did Cody let Seattle hang around with him? Maybe it was because they were both on the track team.

Twice during the morning Billy had a glimpse of Seattle Williams strutting down the hall with two girls. Seattle was good looking, handsome. His dark, wavy hair was always in place. High tight-fitting pants and his loud shirts that showed off his muscles were his trademark in school. He probably could pick out any girl he wanted and go out with her. Billy wished he had half of whatever it was that attracted the girls to Seattle. He didn't know what it was even to hold a girl's hand.

He had about ten minutes left during lunch period when a hand thumped him on the back and a familiar voice startled him out of his reverie. "Hi, Billy. What's the matter? Doesn't anybody want to sit with you?"

Billy looked around, and glanced at both sides of his visitor. "Hi, Seattle. Where are all the girls?"

Seattle laughed. "Why? Want one of them?"

"No."

"Then why'd you ask?"

Billy shrugged. " 'Cause you're hardly around without one."

"I'll get you one. I'll fix you up. How about that?"

"Forget it," insisted Billy, and returned to his lunch. He had only a couple of bites left on a piece of pound cake his mother had baked, and a swallow or two from a pint of milk.

Cody Jones came up and stood beside Seattle. "Well, if it isn't the runner," he quipped. His tone was condescending, tinged with sarcasm.

Billy shrugged off the comment. He was in no mood to have words with Cody Jones. He finished the cake, washed it down with the rest of the milk, and lifted his long legs over the bench.

"I've got to go," he said.

"Billy," Cody cut in, "Seattle tells me he can lose you in his dust in a hundred-yard dash any day of the week. Bet I can too."

"Maybe you can," said Billy, unimpressed.

He paused abruptly as he found himself facing two girls. The red-haired one was Pearl McCarthy; the brunette, Wendy Thaler. Obviously they had heard the tail end of the conversation, and Cody's challenging remark.

Both looked at him intently, but their reactions to what they heard were different. Pearl seemed to have thought the remark was funny. Wendy's eyes seemed to indicate she didn't think it was.

"A lot of legs, but no guts," said Cody.

Billy was looking directly into Wendy's eyes when he heard the cutting remark, so she must have seen the flash of anger in his eyes. Embarrassment flushed his face. If he had ever felt like busting Cody's nose, it was then.

He pivoted on his heels and faced the dark-haired senior. "Okay. You want to race, I'll race."

"Thataway, Billy!" Seattle smiled. "You just might take him, you know. With those long legs you should do the hundred in six strides."

Billy heard him, but his burning eyes were still centered on Cody.

"Name it," he said.

Cody's smile clearly indicated he hadn't a doubt in the world who was going to win the race, no matter what distance they decided it to be.

"Let's run both. The hundred and the two-twenty," he suggested.

"Okay by me."

"Shake on it," Seattle cut in. "Make it legit."

They shook on it.

"May the better man win," Seattle added.

Billy released his grip on Cody's hand, turned, and strode past the girls toward the cafeteria door. He felt their eyes on him, especially Wendy's. For just an instant he had let his eyes meet hers as he brushed by her. He thought he saw something in them that suggested sadness, or sympathy. But at that moment he didn't care what it was. She was one of Seattle's friends, not his.

The afternoon dragged. Billy's classes kept his mind occupied most of the time, away from the thought of the race after school with Cody. But there came moments when he did think of it, and he could feel himself breaking out in a cold sweat.

He was a fool to have accepted Cody's challenge, he thought bitterly. He was sure he was going to lose. He didn't have a chance. He hadn't trained for one hundred or two-hundred-and-twenty-yard dashes.

But he had committed himself; he had to go

through with it. Then the thought crossed his mind that he might beat Cody. If he could put all his power and energy into his two long legs for just the few seconds that it took to run the short distances, he'd do it. Just finishing an inch ahead of Cody was enough.

Dreaming.

The last period seemed to last forever. He found Dan and Sheri in the bus — they both got out of school before he did — and told them not to wait for him, he'd be home later. He didn't explain what was going to delay him, and they didn't press him.

Almost a dozen students besides the racers walked out to the track. Billy noticed Wendy Thaler and Pearl McCarthy among them. And, of course, Seattle Williams, who instigated the whole thing. Billy was nervous, for he knew that Cody was not the kind to shrink from the opportunity to win a bet once he was challenged. He knew he was fast, and that Billy wasn't. He had nothing to lose, and a hungry ego to satisfy.

"Billy, you notice that both of you guys are wearing plain sneakers," said Seattle, as they approached the track. "You can't say that Cody was wearing running shoes and you weren't."

"Thanks for telling me," Billy snorted. He had noticed the minute Cody emerged from the school that he wasn't bringing his track shoes with him. Even Cody would have realized the unfairness in that move.

"You want to warm up a little?" asked Seattle.

"Cody paying you for being his manager?" said Billy.

"Okay, wise guy," Seattle snapped, ignoring the question. "You want to warm up or not?"

"Just a little," Billy said.

He went to the starting line, crouched, then took off, running moderately to get his muscles relaxed and blood circulating. He ran the full one-hundred-yard distance, then trotted back slowly. Cody, he noticed, had just completed a sprint of about twenty yards.

"You guys ready?" Seattle asked.

"Ready," said Billy.

"Ready," Cody echoed.

They got behind the starting line.

"On your mark, get set. Go!" said Seattle.

The runners took off. Cody was ahead almost from the start. The fact that he was wearing long pants instead of racing trunks didn't seem to affect his speed. He was about ten yards ahead of Billy when he zipped across the finish line.

A cheer burst from the small crowd behind them, a small thunder of applause.

"You sure you want to do the two-twenty, too?" Cody asked as he turned, grinning to Billy.

"I said I would, didn't I?" answered Billy, his chest heaving with each breath.

"That's what you said." Cody was breathing only slightly faster than normal.

The two-hundred-and-twenty-yard dash was a disaster. Cody took a large lead, and just when Billy was beginning to narrow the gap a bit, the race was over. Billy lost by fifteen yards. It was, he told himself, worse than he had expected.

He turned to Cody, stuck out his hand for a handshake, and forced a smile.

"Well, you beat me good, Cody," he said. "But you knew I didn't have a chance, didn't you? There'll come a day, though. You wait."

Cody opened his mouth to answer him but cut it short, because Billy had turned away from him and was running across the field in the direction of home.

Chapter 3

HE ARRIVED HOME almost an hour later than he would have if he had ridden on the bus. It was twenty minutes after four and his mother was cooking supper. Billy smelled it the instant he stepped on the front porch.

"Cabbage rolls," he said, recognizing the smell. He stepped into the living room and saw Sheri on the rust-colored rug, changing the dress of her doll. "Hmmm," he went on. "I'm hungry enough to eat a horse."

"Don't look at me!" she exclaimed, looking up at him with wide eyes. "I'm no horse."

"Right. A horse has bigger ears."

He laughed and went through the narrow hall into the kitchen that was filled with the odor of cabbage rolls. His mother was at the gas range, stirring the contents of the large aluminum kettle with a wooden spoon.

"A quarter I can guess what we're having for supper," quipped Billy, giving her a kiss on the cheek.

"I've been waiting for you," she said, ignoring his offer. "The kids said you had to do something so you couldn't come home on the bus. What was it?"

Billy shrugged. "Nothing much."

He lifted the cover of a kettle cooking on another burner. "Corn, great."

"Nothing much?" She stared at his face, at his opened jacket. "You're sweating like a pig. You ran all the way from school, didn't you? What do you want to do? Get sick, too, like your sister?"

He shrugged off his light jacket. "How is Christina?"

"Not better. That medicine helped her cough, but she's got a fever. I'll have to ask you a favor, Billy. I hate to do it, but I don't know what else to do. If just one family had a phone among all these houses it would be simple. I could telephone and there wouldn't be any problem."

"Telephone who?"

"Dr. Shipley. Christina should see him as soon as possible. I don't want her to risk getting bronchitis or pneumonia. They're dangerous illnesses."

"You want me to go after him *now?*"

He held the jacket in a tight roll in his hand, ready to slip it back on if she insisted. He had just run most of the way home from school and was tired and hungry. But he'd go anyway if she wanted him to.

"No," she said. "You can go after supper. I'll have it ready about five-thirty. Why don't you ask Cody to take you? He'll drive you there, I'm sure."

"Cody Jones? Forget it, Mom. I'm not going to ask *him* for anything. Period."

"All right, then. Rest for a while after supper, then go." She looked at him, her blue eyes sorrowed, worried. Christina sure looks like Mom, he suddenly thought. "Maybe one of these days we can move closer to where your father works, into a home where we can have a telephone."

"Can't Dad insist that we need one here?" asked Billy.

"He has. So have other people who live here. But the company is against it. They say that these homes have all been moved once away from the quarry, and that they will be moved again. They don't want to spend the money to run wires up here, and we can't afford to do it on our own. The quarry's expanding."

"The cement company where Dad works says that?"

"Yes. They blasted again today. Everybody had to get out and walk up the field so as not to be struck by falling rocks. But I stayed here with Christina. I couldn't risk getting her out of her warm bed, walking up into the field and waiting for half an hour till they finished blasting. I just sat close beside her all the time and prayed to God that no rock would fall on our house. None did."

Billy stared at her as he conjured the picture in his mind that she painted so graphically for him. He knew what she was talking about. There was dynamite blasting in the quarry in the summertime, too. He hated the loud, eerie whine of the siren that warned the inhabitants of the company-owned stucco homes to get out and walk up into the field above them where they could be assured of safety from flying, falling rocks.

It was infrequent that a large falling rock, big enough to crash through the roof of a home, ever found a target. But almost every home had been hit one time or another, and sometimes by a rock that had plunged through the roof and ceiling, and even through the floor. A life had never been lost, but a boy had been hit by falling debris some years back, before the danger of remaining in the homes during a blasting had been noticed. Ever since then the company had issued a proclamation that every home had to be vacated at the sound of the warning siren. There was a fifty-dollar fine levied if the order was disobeyed.

"It's ridiculous to live like this," said Billy, sprawling in a chair. "Why don't we move the heck out of here?"

"Can't. Not for a while. Rent is real cheap here. And your father's earnings aren't enough to pay the higher rent of a better home, or to buy a house yet. Anyway, we're saving money. Every week your father has money taken out of his check that goes into a savings account. When we have enough to put a down payment on a house, we're going to get out. We must just be patient."

She glanced at the wall clock. "Look for Dan, will you, please, Billy? I swear he hasn't been in the house for five minutes since he got home from school. I've never seen such a kid. Always on the go."

Billy got to his feet and put his jacket back on. "He say where he was going? I hope he's not fighting again."

"Who knows where he goes? He doesn't know himself until he gets there."

Dan had mostly his father's characteristics. He was short and stocky, with more energy than most two boys put together. But, unlike his father, Dan still had not developed control over his temper. He seemed to think fighting went along with the growing process.

Billy's fear that his younger brother might be entangled in another scrap turned out to have a basis.

He found a human arena at the softball diamond that the kids had laid out in the field separating the quarry from the homes. In the middle of it two kids were going at it furiously. One was almost a foot taller than the other, and taking the worst of the beating. The smaller one had on a blue shirt with sleeves rolled up above his elbows. Billy had a feeling that when Dan was old enough he'd join the navy and have a tattoo burned on each bicep.

Billy's long legs churned as fast as he could get them to as he headed toward the fight. "Hey, you guys! Stop it!" he yelled. "Stop it! You hear me?"

Some of the small crowd heard him and turned, saw him coming, and quickly related the message to the fighters. The battle continued; neither gladiator paid any attention to him.

All at once only the shorter of the two was standing. Dan. He stood above his fallen opponent, fists still clenched, chest heaving, jaws squared.

"Dan!" Billy said, plunging through the ring of onlookers. "Man, what're you fighting about now?"

Dan looked around at him, a mischievous gleam of pride in his victory dancing in his brown eyes. Wordlessly, he scooped up his jacket which was lying on the ground and started to go through the line.

Billy grabbed his arm. "That kid's hurt. He's still lying there. What started the fight, I asked you?"

"Dan was blocking home plate and Steve ran into him," one of the softball players explained.

"He could've slid. But he didn't," Dan declared. He shrugged Billy's hand off his shoulder and walked through the line that opened up like an automatic door for him.

Billy headed for the loser of the fight, but Steve was rising to his feet under his own power. There were a couple of small bruises on his face, and his shirt was torn.

"You okay, Steve?" asked Billy, brushing dirt off the tall boy's pants.

"Never mind. I'm all right," Steve said, drawing away from him.

Most of the onlookers seemed obviously pleased that they had had a ringside look to a good fight, even if it was one-sided.

Billy followed his brother home, wondering what the future would hold for the tough little rascal. Maybe he'd wind up a boxer. Who could really tell? Using his fists so adeptly at this stage could mean a fighting career, and a good one, too.

Billy shook his head. He knew that if Dan became a fighter, and he got good at running, his parents would have a fit. Neither one of them viewed athletics as anything more than fun games. Although a career in the ring could bring in instant money, a fast runner in high school could be offered a college scholarship. If he was very good, the Olympics could be his ultimate goal. A gold medal — or even a silver medal — could open doors for him into a career that even Mom and Dad would joyously respect.

There was no avoiding the reason for the glum look on Dan's face. Even though there were no physical signs that he'd been in a scrap, his face showed that he had been in some kind of trouble. Billy got him off the hook by telling his mother just part of what had happened, that a kid had run into Dan at home plate and you can't carry a smile on your face under such circumstances now, can you? His mother said no, I guess you can't, and the matter was dropped.

Billy hung up his jacket and went to see Christina. She had her eyes closed as he entered the room, but opened them the minute he approached the bed. A weak smile flickered over her pale face.

"Hi," she greeted him.

"Hi, Chris. How you feeling?"

"Not too good. Mom said you're going after Dr. Shipley after supper."

"Yes. She thinks you'll get better quicker if he sees you."

"Are you going to walk? He must live at least three or four miles away."

Billy shrugged. "Maybe I'll be lucky. Maybe somebody will pick me up."

He sat on the edge of the bed, crossed his arms over his chest and smiled at her. Seeing the other kids up and around without her was like looking at a chain with a missing link. In a way she was like Dan. She enjoyed being on the go, playing softball with the boys, playing pitch and catch when there weren't enough players for a game, swimming at the pond on Mitch Wendell's farm. But she didn't have Dan's temper, and Billy was thankful for that.

After supper he sat around for fifteen minutes, then put on his jacket and started out on a run to Dr. Shipley's house on Haden Road. He wasn't lucky. He had to run all the way.

Chapter 4

"YOU RAN ALL THE WAY?" Mrs. Shipley asked, her brow furrowed.

"Yes," said Billy.

"What a shame. Isn't there anyone living there who has a car?"

"Oh, yes. But I don't mind."

No point in telling her that Cody Jones had a car. She'd want to know why he hadn't asked Cody, and he'd have to explain about the stupid game that Cody and Seattle had played on him while he was running home in the rain that day, and then his refusal to accept a ride when the game was over. It seemed so childish now, and Mrs. Shipley would surely think so, too.

"You'll wait now, won't you?" she asked, looking warmly at Billy. She was in her sixties, a short, silver-haired woman who seemed as full of vitality as one twenty years younger. "The doctor was called out on an emergency about an hour ago, so I think he should be coming home shortly. Then you can ride back with him."

"Okay," said Billy.

"Take a seat," she invited. "People start coming in about a quarter of seven for their appointments. But that's still half an hour away. Would you like to have something to drink? Tea or lemonade?"

"No, thanks."

Dr. Shipley arrived within the next fifteen minutes. Billy explained about Christina and, because the doctor said he had to be back to attend to the patients who had appointments, he hurried out to his car with Billy at his heels, started it up, backed it out of the driveway, and sped down the road.

Billy had managed to get the mileage on the odometer before the car had started rolling and hoped he'd remember to look at it again when they arrived at his home. He wanted to see how far he had run.

"Haven't seen you for some time, Billy," said the doctor. He was a big man, over six feet tall and at least two hundred pounds. "What grade are you in, Billy? Tenth? Eleventh?"

"Ninth," said Billy. "I'm only fourteen."

"Right. I should have remembered. Any ambitions for the future? Or is it too early yet to predict what you're going to do when you really grow up?"

"It's pretty early," replied Billy.

"Well, yes, it is. Are you into sports at all?"

32

"Not yet. But I will be."

"You haven't played basketball?" The doctor looked at him, his square-jawed face showing mild surprise. "You've got the height. I should think that would be your game."

"No. I played a little, is all. I just don't care for it, I guess."

"Well, nothing wrong with that." A smile deepened the wrinkles at the corners of the doctor's eyes. "Mrs. Shipley told me that you ran all the way from your home to my office. That's quite a run."

"I looked at the odometer when I got in the car," admitted Billy. "I'm anxious to see just exactly how far it is."

"Good idea. Have you considered track? That's a good field, you know. It has tremendous potential. If you were really good you might win a scholarship to a university, then study for a career that will set you up nicely for the rest of your life. Other sports provide the same opportunity, of course, but —" he smiled again as he cast another sidewise glance at Billy "— I can't quite picture you as an up and coming baseball or football great. What do you think?"

"I think you're right," said Billy, who had never had any ambitions of playing either one of those sports, anyway.

When the car stopped in front of his home he

looked at the odometer again, and quickly calculated that they had driven three and two-tenths miles. Without stopping once, that wasn't a bad run, in his opinion.

The doctor remained with Christina only about ten minutes. He left pills for her to take, and said she should be well and on her feet again in two or three days. Meanwhile, it was best that she rested.

After the doctor left, and the door was closed to Christina's room, Sam Chekko made an announcement that stopped the whole family in its tracks.

"Family, I'm going to buy us a car," he said. "I'm sick and tired of this business of begging for rides, of Billy running here and there for groceries, for the doctor, for anything."

Surprised, they all stared at him. Dan's and Sheri's faces were glowing from thoughts of the wonderful things that the possession of a car would bring them. His wife didn't seem to know what to make of it. This was the first time since they were married that her husband had made up his mind about something important so quickly, and she wondered if her ears were deceiving her. Billy was dumbfounded, but pleased. If a car in the family was going to relieve anyone of a tiresome task, it would be him.

"With what?" Mrs. Chekko asked, after she had managed to get over her surprise.

"What do you mean 'with what?' " Mr. Chekko said, staring at her. "I'm not going to buy a *new* car. I'm thinking of one about three or four years old. I'll take the down payment out of our savings and pay the balance in installments. Two or three years, whatever they give us. In that way we won't have to fork out too much money every month. Don't you think it's a good idea, Adelia?"

She shrugged, then went up to him and planted a kiss on his lips. It was a gesture that none of the kids saw very often between their mother and father, and it amused them. Sheri ran up to them and swung her small arms around their legs, her tiny fists clenching the cloth of her father's pants and her mother's dress.

Billy held his breath for a few moments, surprised that he could be so close to tears. Before he could see how Dan was reacting to the situation, his brother turned and went quietly into the living room.

"Hey, Danny," Billy called to him. "What do you think of that, huh? Imagine having a car after *never* having one!"

Dan plopped himself on a chair, sprawled out his legs and folded his hands over his stomach. "I think it's about time," he said. "Maybe now we can see a movie once in a while."

Moments later Mr. and Mrs. Chekko and Sheri came into the room. Mrs. Chekko had her arm around her husband's waist. The smile still lingered on her lips.

"You know what getting a car means, Dad?" asked Billy. "You'll have to learn to drive. Did you ever drive a car?"

"Why, sure! But a long time ago. I had a driver's license for five or six years."

"Then what happened?"

"I lost it."

"Lost it? How?"

He grinned shyly. "I had an accident, and my license was revoked for six months. I never renewed it. I sold the car and never bought another one."

"Was that before you were married to Mom?"

"We'd been married a year," he answered. "Okay, let's drop the subject. It wasn't one of my best years."

"Oh — it *wasn't?*" his wife said, looking directly at him, her nose only inches away from his face.

"Oh, I didn't mean it *that* way!" he exclaimed. "I'm talking about the car, sweetheart!"

Everyone laughed. For a few moments longer the kids teased their father about his statement which his wife had twisted into a joke on himself, but they stopped abruptly when they remembered that there was a sick girl in another room who required rest and quiet.

That night Billy dreamed that he was running

through a quagmire that was up to his ankles. Seattle, Cody, and some of the school kids were running ahead of him. None of them seemed to be having the difficulty he was. He was trailing far behind, and losing ground with every hard, grinding step. His calves, heels, and toes were aching terribly. He could see his own face, as if he were looking into a mirror, screwed up with strain as he tried to break loose from the quagmire and catch up with the runners far in front of him. He grunted, groaned, even shouted out loud to vent his anger.

He woke up, cold with sweat.

There was a bunch of students — mostly boys — standing in front of the bulletin board in the main corridor the next morning as Billy headed for his classroom. He immediately recognized Seattle Williams, Luke Maynard, Rudy Joy and two others whom he knew were interested in track. Did whatever they were reading have something to do with that?

He walked up behind them and, after quickly scanning over some of the announcements, saw the one he expected. It was a sign-up sheet for the track team, issued by the track coach, Roland Seavers. The participants were also asked to write the event, or events, of their choice.

There were half a dozen names on it already. Seattle signed up next, then Luke. Billy saw that Rudy's name headed the list, his choices being the eight-eighty, the mile, and the two-mile races.

"Hi, Billy," he said, glancing around at the boy who was about four inches taller than he. "You going to put your name on that? We can use your long legs."

Billy shrugged.

Seattle, turning away from the board, flashed a smile at him.

"Billy boy!" he cried. "Here, use my pen and sign your John Hancock up there, man. Maybe you'll turn out to be the broad-jump champion of Cove Hill Central!"

"No, thanks," said Billy.

The smile faded from Seattle's face. "You're not going to sign up?"

Billy's answer was only a shrug. If you're so interested in knowing whether I'm going to sign up or not, pal, he thought, I'll just let you wait and wonder. It's about time I played a little game on you.

"Man, you're real talkative today, aren't you?" said Seattle. "What's the matter? Cody scare you out of it by beating you in the hundred and two-twenty yesterday?" His eyes danced for a moment. "When it comes to sprints, he and I are just the greatest, man. Didn't you know that?"

Most of the small crowd broke out laughing, except one of the girls standing at its rim to the right of Billy. She didn't seem to find anything funny in Seattle's remark. On the contrary, from the somewhat disgusted look on Wendy Thaler's face, she might have considered it downright obnoxious.

Billy felt the condescension in the remark, but tried not to show that it bothered him. Everyone knew of Seattle's boasting stories; whether anyone believed them was something else. Seattle had come from Seattle, Washington, and used to tell of his exploits there, in baseball, track, even with girls, till the kids at Cove Hill stuck him with the nickname, Seattle. In the last year or so his memory of all the wonderful things he had done in that city seemed to have deteriorated. But Billy figured that Seattle's loss of memory was mostly due to the teasing he got from the kids.

Billy started to walk away, and soon realized that someone was coming up beside him. To his surprise he saw it was Wendy.

"What are you doing here?" he asked.

"Can't I walk with you?" she said, catching up to him.

"Yes, but —" He shrugged.

"If you'd slow down just a little bit, maybe I'd be able to walk alongside you."

He blushed and slowed down his pace. He felt like a giant beside her.

"You in track?" he asked. "That's for girls, too, I noticed."

"No," she said. "But I like to watch. How come you didn't sign up?"

"I will."

"I hope you're not going to let that wise guy affect your decision."

"Seattle? I thought he was one of your friends."

"He's all right. At times. But I don't like a guy who blows his own horn too much."

"He's cocky, but he lives up to it. He's no phony."

She offered no comment.

They were approaching the classroom he had to enter, and he slowed down, wanting to let these few precious seconds last as long as possible. He found he liked her. She was friendly, soft-spoken, intelligent without being snooty about it.

It wasn't till they were at the door of the room and he stopped and looked at her that she spoke again.

"I think you could make a good runner, Billy," she

said brightly. "Cove Hill can use someone besides a sprinter. There's more to track than just the one-hundred-dred dash, you know."

"Yes," he agreed. "I know."

Chapter 5

HE PUT HIS SIGNATURE on the list shortly after the end of the first afternoon period, adding the eight-eighty, one mile, and two-mile to it, the same as Rudy had done.

Looking around he hoped he would see Wendy, but he didn't. A river of humanity was flowing by him, and there were cheerful calls to him from classmates and others who knew who he was because of his height. He was the tallest ninth grader in school. Every time he walked in the corridor he was conscious of it. Very few older kids — sophomores, juniors or seniors — were taller than he.

Wendy was in his algebra class, and flashed him a brief smile when their eyes met. But when they had an opportunity to talk she made no effort to, and he assumed that she hadn't checked the board yet, didn't know he had signed up.

It wasn't till the end of third period that he was accosted in the corridor by Seattle and some of the other guys who had signed up for track. Seattle held out both hands, waiting for Billy to give him two fives. Billy did, and he loudly exclaimed, "Billy! You signed up! Thataboy, man! Now Rudy won't have to worry about being tailend Charlie anymore! Ha! Ha!"

Billy felt like flattening Seattle's nose against that smooth-skinned, smug face of his that so many girls thought was so beautiful.

"What do you mean I've been tailend Charlie?" cried Rudy, pretending hurt. "I was tailend Charlie only twice last year! Check the records, man!"

"Don't lose your cool, ol' buddy," said Seattle, patting him on the back. "Don't you recognize a figure of speech when you hear one?"

"I'm lousy in English," Rudy quipped.

By Monday morning Christina was well enough to go back to school. She was slightly pale and looked as if she had lost some weight, but because she had been on the plump side anyway, her mother told her she looked good. What she had missed mostly, she told the kids on the bus, was playing field hockey during the noon hours.

Billy read a notice on the bulletin board that announced a meeting of the track team right after school. The boys were to meet at the south end of the track with Coach Roland Seavers, and the girls at the north end with Coach Sue Callahan.

A swarm of enthusiastic athletes showed up. Uniforms were distributed. Most of them were old, but there were some new ones that replaced the ones that were torn or worn too badly to appear in public again.

Billy saw that the uniform given to him was almost ready for the scrap pile, too. But he accepted it willingly, figuring that he had to earn his spurs before he'd qualify for a brand new one. Among the five or six pairs of old track shoes he tried on he found one that fitted him. It was a snug fit but he didn't complain.

Seattle, Luke, and Rudy were given new uniforms. Rudy? Billy asked himself. Was he that good that he deserved a new uniform?

The coach called the team together. He was about five-ten, wore a blue baseball cap, a gray sweatshirt, and gray sweatpants. From the minute he started to talk Billy knew that he was a tough, hard-as-nails, no-holds-barred coach who spat out words as if they were lead pellets and meant to hit the target with every one of them.

"If you don't know me yet, I'm your coach, Roland Seavers," he bellowed. "I expect you to address me as Coach Seavers, or just Coach. The gentleman at my right," he pointed to a tall, angular man beside him, "is my assistant, Dick Rafini. You'll also address him as Coach." He cleared his throat. "I'm not an old man but I have old-fashioned ideas. I like to win. Maybe some of you think that isn't so old-fashioned. Well, you're right. Some schools are satisfied to have a track team just so the alumni can reminisce about it at the sports banquets. But I want a winner. I want Cove Hill to have a track team that will bring home trophies. I want Cove Hill to have a track team that the school will be just as proud of as they are of its baseball and football teams. That's a status we haven't been able to gain yet. It's a damn shame that a school like ours can't pick up more wins. It's a reflection on your school. It's a reflection on me. But a coach can only get out of his team what it gives him.

"Track is an individual sport, but it's also team-work. Hell, I don't have to tell you that. But you'd be surprised how many of you think it isn't. You put on your trunks and track shoes, come out here, work out, and seem so bushed you look like a field of dried-up vegetables. I'm talking about last year, the year before and the year before that." His eyes hardened. "You work out to get in condition and *stay* in condition. No staying up late at night. No heavy eating. Only two or three of you put in enough effort to indicate that you've got at least part of your heart in it. Well, this year I want more. I'm not *asking* you; I'm *telling* you. *Give me all you've got or hand in your trunks.* I'm fed up with being on the bottom of our athletic totem pole every year. I want this team to climb up this year. And I know we can do it if you get off your butts and give it all you've got." He paused, cleared his throat.

"I think that Jones will still be the league's best sprinter for the sixty and one hundred yarders. He should do pretty well, too, in the two-twenty. But I'd like to see a guy or two push us ahead in the hurdles, the eight-eighty, the mile, and the two-mile. Colloni still has the edge on the discus. When he graduates this year we'll be back in the shadows in that department, unless our rivals lose their best throwers, too."

While he was talking his eyes were sweeping over his prospects, and a couple of times Billy felt them pause for just a moment on him. Now suddenly they were on him again. They held a challenge so strong and alive he wanted to tear his eyes away.

"You, there. Chekko. Billy Chekko, right?"

Billy nodded, embarrassed that he was singled out like this.

"How tall are you, Chekko?"

"Six-foot-one."

"Tenth grade?"

"Ninth."

The coach frowned. "Ninth? How old are you?"

46

"Fourteen."

"Fourteen?" A smile rippled over the coach's face. "You listen to me, Chekko, and maybe Cove Hill will start making waves." He looked back at the rest of the squad. Billy sighed, glad to be out of the spotlight. "Okay! Spread out for some routine calisthenics! After that, Mr. Rafini and I will divide you up into the various categories, put you in spots that I will judge you're best suited for, no matter what you wrote as your choices. All right? All right!"

Coach Seavers led the calisthenics, but Mr. Rafini, about five yards to his left, went through the routines with him and the team. Pushups, situps, jumps. "One! Two! One! Two! One! Two!"

Ten minutes of this, then a two-minute rest period. Then exercises again.

After half an hour they all lay on the ground, chests heaving, every muscle screaming with pain. Billy lay limp, his long arms and legs stretched out, his sweating face turned to the sky, his eyes closed. He had thought that all the running he had done would have prepared him for this, but he hadn't realized there were muscles that were hardly used while running. Fortunately his chest didn't feel the torture that his arms and shoulders did. But his stomach muscles were like knotted ropes. Oh, man! And this was only the first day!

Afterward they all ran sprints on the grassy field, stopping when they heard Coach Seavers blow his whistle. It was a loud, shrill sound, lasting for about two seconds, dying abruptly.

Billy hadn't thought about what position he had finished in, because he didn't think it mattered. But Coach Seavers apparently did.

"Chekko! Quit dragging your ass! For a long bean you should be somewhere near the front, not last!"

Billy's neck turned beet red. Nobody laughed at the remark, but he saw some of them snicker, amused by their coach's pungent outburst.

"All right! Let's go through it again!" barked the coach.

A few grudging remarks dropped, but the coach either hadn't heard them or was totally ignoring them. The guys lined up again, Billy about two-thirds from the left end of the line. They waited for the whistle, then took off when it shrilled. Billy's legs churned as he tried to run faster than he had before, knowing now that the coach was watching him.

"Pick up your legs, Chekko!" came his resounding yell.

"Faster, man! Faster!"

After Billy was sure they had covered at least a hundred yards he waited for the sound of the whistle again. He had reached the peak of his speed some ten or fifteen yards back, and he knew he had slowed down. Why didn't the coach blow that damn whistle?

Then he heard it slice the air, a rippling scream that pierced his eardrums as if the coach were standing much closer to him than he actually was. The boys as one stopped running. Some collapsed on the spot, dead tired. Billy felt like doing so, too, but stayed on his feet, waiting for the coach to single him out again with another raw remark.

"Chekko! Come here!"

Billy turned and headed toward him without looking up. Sweat drenched his hair and face, dripped into his eyes. His heart thundered in his ears.

"Look at me, Chekko."

Billy was within seven or eight feet of him now, his eyes still looking down at the grass. At the coach's order he glanced up, meeting the direct stare squarely.

"You run like a stumble bum, Chekko. You're not picking up your feet." The coach paused, as if waiting for that morsel of information to sink in. He went on gruffly, "Lift those knees. Bring them up high. Touch the ground with the balls of your feet *first*. You've got the height to make it, Chekko.

You've got the reach. All you've got to do is develop speed, and if you'll listen to me you will. Do you hear me, Chekko?"

"Every word, Coach," said Billy, looking at the coach through the sweat that blurred his eyes.

He was hurt, humiliated. Probably every ear there had heard that blistering chewing out.

"It's for the good of all of us that I'm telling you this, Chekko. And I want to tell you this now, before we get too far into this thing. I don't want a communication gap between us. Understand? If you have anything to say, say it. If you don't, just keep your ears open and do as I say. Do you hear me, Chekko?"

"I hear you, Coach," said Billy.

"Fine. Okay, guys!" the coach turned and yelled to the athletes scattered on the field. "Tomorrow! Here! Same time! Any questions?"

Nobody said a word.

"Dismissed," he said, and headed toward the school, his strides short and rapid. Billy wondered how the guy could have so much energy.

He started to head for the school too, when he heard soft footsteps pounding on the turf behind him. "Hey, wait a minute!" a voice called.

It was Wendy. Why do you have to be here? he thought angrily. Aren't I humiliated enough without your being around to hear it all? He said, "Hi," to her, but kept walking toward the school without slowing his gait. The faster he got away from her the better.

"You don't have to act so angry," she said, hurrying to catch up with him. "He talks like that to most of the guys."

"How do you know?" he said. "Don't you even miss one of these practices?"

He sounded bitter, and he tried to tell himself that he was justified. Maybe the coach talks like that to most of the guys, he thought, but this is the first time he talked like that to me. The abuse and humiliation were new to him. He hadn't had time to build up a resistance to them yet.

"Sorry," she said. "I guess I'm not wanted here."

He saw her stop and turn away. He stopped too and turned around, trying quickly to think of how to say that he was also sorry. There was only the one direct way. "Wendy, I'm sorry!"

But she was running away from him.

You boob, he said disgustedly to himself. You sure blew it this time.

Chapter 6

BILLY ADJUSTED THE SHOWER to a lukewarm spray, wetted and lathered himself with soap, then turned slowly round and round underneath the gushing water till he was thoroughly rinsed.

Feeling fresh and clean, he toweled himself and dressed, refusing to become involved in the silly conversations that had sprung up among the other members of the track and field squad. He recognized Seattle's voice addressing him, making some kind of remark about him and Wendy, and anger flared up inside him. But he fought to control himself, fearing that being intimidated now might result in something foolish.

Something foolish? Like what? He didn't like arguments. He could never think of things to say, not till much later when he had time to think. And he didn't like fist fights. He was no Danny. He didn't believe in settling an argument with fists.

The door of the locker room closed behind him with a soft *whoosh!* The yellow bus was parked at the curb, the driver already in it, reading a paper.

He greeted Billy as the boy climbed up into the bus.

"Hi, Mr. Corey," said Billy, and headed for a seat toward the back. He dropped his duffel bag on the floor and sat down, made himself comfortable in the corner, and closed his eyes.

The kids started to pile in, and one of them sat down beside him and spoke to him. He just opened his eyes to identify his companion, said "Hi" to him, and closed his eyes again. He recalled nothing till the kid next to him shook him awake and said, "Hey, Billy. Wake up. You're home."

"I didn't know you were staying after school to practice track," said his mother indignantly. "Why didn't you say something?"

Billy shoved the duffel bag against the wall. "I thought I told you," he said. "I'm sorry."

"You going to leave that bag there? Put it in the closet."

"The suit needs washing, Mom," he said. "It's pretty smelly."

"Then take it out and put it in the hamper."

"I need it again tomorrow," he said.

She looked at him. Her hair was slightly tousled, and her face sweaty. She was in the process of cooking supper for her family of six — he could smell the chicken — but sometime during the day she must have vacuumed the rugs or washed clothes or done something else that made her look so tired.

"Never mind, Mom," he said. "I'll wash it myself. I'll let it soak in the small tub for a while, then wash it good with soap and water." He went and emptied the bag. "Where are the kids?" he asked.

"I'm here!" said Christina, emerging from the dining room.

"Hey," said Billy, smiling, "you look pretty healthy to me. How did school go?"

"Okay." Her eyes sparkled. "I guess I'll have to get sick again sometime."

"What do you mean?"

"I never realized how many friends I had. It was just great." Her cheeks glowed, reflecting the joy that must have been bubbling inside her.

"Listen, kid," said Billy. "Anybody that doesn't like you has a hole in his head. Take it from me, your big brother."

"Okay, big brother," his mother cut in. "She's taken it. Now you take that stuff you have there in your hands and start soaking it before it smells up this whole kitchen. You know where the tub is?"

"In the closet?"

"Right. Hanging on the wall. A box of detergent sets on the shelf above it. Fill the tub half full and just put a tablespoonful of the detergent into it. Think you can do that?"

"Oh, Mom," he said.

He had the uniform soaking in the tub on the back porch when he heard someone crying outside and realized it was his younger sister. He looked out of the window, saw her coming up the porch, and went and opened the door for her.

"Sheri!" he exclaimed, looking her over for bruises in case she had fallen. "What happened to you?"

"Danny slapped me!" she sobbed.

"Danny did? Why?"

"He took the trike from me!"

One small fist rubbing an eye, the other trembling slightly at her side, she continued on through the next door into the kitchen. It wasn't the first time that she and Dan had come to blows over something, and not the first time she lost out. The tire hanging by a rope from the gnarled old oak tree in the back yard had been the cause of trouble between them several times.

"I don't know about that Dan," Billy grumbled, as he dried his hands on a towel and headed in long strides toward the door. "I've got a good notion to kick him in the fanny one of these days for picking on his little sister."

He found his younger brother riding the tricycle on the path leading toward the garden beyond the grassless, lumpy yard. The vehicle was a model big enough for Sheri but hardly large enough to accommodate Dan. To pedal it he had to keep his knees bent outward so that they wouldn't bang up against the handlebars. But he didn't let this minor problem stop him from riding the tricycle around the place as fast as he could pedal it. It was a miracle, thought Billy, that Dan was able to maintain his balance.

"Dan!" Billy shouted at him. "You big horse! Get off that trike before you ruin it!"

"Who said I'll ruin it?" said Dan, not showing any fear of his older brother.

"I did!"

Billy ran across the yard toward Dan, anger flashing in his eyes. But before he got within ten feet of Dan, the younger boy stopped the trike and looked directly into his brother's eyes unflinchingly.

"I heard her say I slapped her," he said. "She's a liar. I didn't slap her."

"Okay. You didn't slap her. I know she tells tall tales sometimes." The anger dissipated. He was once again brother, not just big brother. "But that trike's too small for you, Dan. You'll really ruin it riding it the way you were. Talk to Dad about getting you a two-wheeler. Maybe he'll get you a secondhand one."

"I have."

"What did he say?"

"Someday."

"Well? He promised, didn't he?"

"Sure." The tone of his voice suggested that "someday" could mean a hundred years from now.

"Supper's ready!" came a cry from the back-porch door.

Billy laid an arm over his brother's shoulders as they headed toward the house. He guessed that he would never be surprised at whatever Dan might do, whether it was a good thing or bad. One thing seemed certain about him: he was a fearless cuss.

Before they reached the back porch a movement out of the corner of his eye caught Billy's attention. He turned quickly and saw two boys in white trunks running on the road. He recognized them instantly. Luke Maynard and Rudy Joy.

They exchanged greetings, and in a moment were out of sight as they passed behind the house.

"That Maynard kid has a brother in my class," said Dan. "He told me that Luke's in the cross-country. Maybe you'd be better in that, Billy."

Billy stared at him. "What do you mean maybe I'd be better in that? Don't you think I'm good in what I want to run?"

Their eyes clinched, then Dan looked away, his mouth opening but not releasing any words.

"You heard some of your friends talking about me? Is that it, Dan?" Billy asked.

Dan shrugged. "Yeah."

They had reached the porch by now, and Billy paused to let Dan go ahead of him.

"Dan."

Dan glanced up at his taller brother.

Billy grinned. "Let 'em talk. This kid's going to be a runner one of these days." He jabbed his right thumb hard against his own chest as he spoke. "Before the season's over they'll be talking out of the other side of their mouths. You wait and see."

"Sure. I'll wait," said Dan.

"You don't believe me, do you?"

"Sure I believe you. When I see it," Dan said, and went up on the porch.

Billy was silent during the meal. Chicken and dumplings was one of his favorites, but his appetite had been diminished by Dan's honest and unbiased opinion of his potential as a runner. If Dan felt he had no chance in running races other than the cross-country, a lot of other kids might feel the same way.

But what could running the cross-country prove? That a runner had plenty of endurance? Of stamina?

So what? He had to have endurance and stamina in any kind of run.

He had a second helping, nevertheless. Second helpings were almost always automatic for him, whether or not he had an upset stomach.

"We're going to the woods to cut down some trees for firewood," his father announced at the table. "So don't you boys plan on running off. Okay?"

"Okay," said Billy. There was no comment from Dan. Cutting down trees, chopping off the branches, and sawing off pieces to carrying size didn't appeal to him. That was work, not fun.

Billy didn't exactly love it either. But he had a different outlook on the hand-blistering, grueling task now. The hard work would help build up his body, condition his legs for the running he was going to do. The running he *had* to do to prove himself.

Chapter 7

BILLY WAS AT ONE END of the long saw, his father at the other. The tall pine they were cutting down was about a foot thick at the trunk, but the saw ate through it hungrily as father and son pushed and pulled at a slow, steady pace.

Billy liked the tart smell of the pine, the beauty of the cones, and everything else about the woods. There was no name that he knew of for the hundreds of acres of wooded land. All he knew was what his father knew, that it was owned by the cement company where his father worked and that the company permitted their tenants to cut down the trees for firewood. Two rules prevailed: that the woods be kept clean, and that the cut wood be used on the tenants' premises. Selling it was forbidden.

Billy felt his arms tiring. Now and then he glanced at his father, noticing his sweating face and his attentive eyes riveted upon the gnawing saw. The muscles bulged in his short, hairy arms. Billy wished he had even one half of his father's strength.

When there were two to three inches left to saw,

Mr. Chekko said, "Okay. Enough. I'll use the axe to fell her. Stand back, both of you."

Billy and Dan went and stood behind their father. When they were a safe distance away Mr. Chekko wielded the axe, the sharp edge cutting deep into the bark opposite the sawed side. First a slant from the top, then from the bottom, while the chips flew. Then he gave a yell, "There it goes!" and jumped back a couple of steps. Other trees had been felled in the area, so this fresh one crashed down unhindered upon the dead leaves on the earth.

Now the chore fell upon Billy and Dan to saw short pieces from the main trunk while their father chopped off the branches. It took only a few minutes of work before Dan was sweating too. Billy forced frequent rests when he saw that the effort was tiring Dan. He didn't want his brother to become so discouraged with the job that he'd carry a grudge the rest of the evening, even though he was amply sure that Dan wouldn't quit no matter how tired he became. He was too proud to ever throw in the towel.

The boys and their father made two trips each to their back yard, Billy and Dan carrying a log between them while their father carried one himself. Billy figured that the one his father carried weighed about as much as the one he and Dan carried together.

"Okay. That'll be enough for today," said Mr.

Chekko. "We'll fetch some more home tomorrow."

Billy felt his hands burn, looked at his palms, and saw the opened blisters.

"Look at mine," said Dan. Billy did, and saw the small, husky hands red as his own, with opened blisters, too.

"How do you expect to run if Dad keeps us working every day after he gets home from work?" asked Dan as the brothers headed toward the house from the yard where they had piled up the logs.

"I've got to manage it somehow," replied Billy.

"You'll never make a runner, Billy," Dan said seriously. "Never."

"Dan!" Billy stared at his brother incredulously. "I — I can't believe you said that!"

"Dad doesn't want you to run," said Dan. "You know what he told Mom?"

"What?"

"Good athletes don't go in for running. They play tougher sports, like football, baseball, basketball —"

"Baloney!"

"Tell that to Dad," said Dan.

He opened the door of the back porch and they walked in. Billy turned briefly to look back at his father who had remained behind to clean up the area where additional logs were to be placed.

A bitter light entered his eyes. So good athletes don't go in for running, huh, Dad? That's how much you know about it. Nothing. All athletes run, Dad. Did you ever hear of the International Amateur Athletic Federation? World track and field competition is governed by it.

Did you know that there's been professional track and field in the United States since the early 1970s?

Billy agreed with his father that running wasn't like football, baseball, or basketball. Nor was it even like hockey or tennis. But it was still what he wanted to do, because he enjoyed it. It was going to help build up his skinny body, put meat on his skinny bones, develop some of that meat into hard muscle. It was going to make him into something else, too. A *somebody*. Just like it made Jim Ryun somebody. And John Walker somebody. Jim Ryun won the one-mile race in 3 minutes 51.1 seconds for the United States in 1967. John Walker won it in 3 minutes 49.4 for New Zealand in 1975. They competed for world titles, just like Muhammad Ali did. Just like the Yankees and the Dodgers did.

That's the star he was shooting for. To be somebody. Maybe later on, when he graduated from high school and maybe college, he'd change his sights to a different star. But today it was to be a great runner.

Because his father needed him to help with more

cutting of the tree, plus felling a second and a third, Billy missed the next day of practice. It worried him what Coach Seavers might say to him when he resumed practice. But wood was a necessity, and it was free for the taking. Procuring it had to be done. Maybe the coach would understand that — and maybe he wouldn't.

It was on Wednesday morning that Billy saw Coach Seavers in the hall. The coach was alone, carrying a book in his hand, and walking at a brisk pace, as if he were in a hurry to get somewhere. Wearing a blue blazer, a striped tie, and light gray slacks, he looked altogether different from the person in coach togs who commanded his track and field squad like an army general.

It was between periods when students were changing classes, so the corridor was crowded. Billy eased over toward the side in the hope that the farther away he got from the coach the greater the possibility was that the coach wouldn't see him.

He was right. At least he thought he was, since the coach didn't glance at him once, speaking only to those students who passed close by him and spoke to him.

Billy knew it was just a moment's respite. If he didn't meet the coach face to face in the hall, he'd meet him on the field.

He wasn't able to keep out of sight of Seattle and Rudy, though, and their taunting remarks.

"What did you do, quit?" asked Seattle. "Can't take it?"

"He hates to come out on the tail end all the time," grinned Rudy. "Can't blame him."

"I didn't quit," Billy said emphatically. "I had work to do."

"Work? You got a part-time job or something?" Seattle seemed to be having a delightful time jibing him.

Rudy grabbed Billy's hand, but Billy yanked it away from him before Rudy could see the calloused, open-blistered palm.

"I saw you carrying wood," said Rudy. "You and Dan and your old man. That the work you talking about?"

"That's the work," Billy said.

"Maybe that's what you're cut out for, Billy," said Seattle. "A lumberjack. Timberrrrrr!"

Billy walked away, bristling with anger, the sound of Seattle's and Rudy's laughter echoing behind him.

After school he took the early bus home again to help his father saw down a tree, cut it into about five-foot lengths, carry them to their back yard, saw them to shorter lengths, then chop them and neatly stack up the kindling-size wood in a tall, round pile. Dan helped, too. And Christina, wearing blue jeans, a warm jacket, and gloves, worked alongside her brothers and father as hard and steadily as they, the sweat rolling down her nose and cheeks.

"Good job, kids," their father praised them when the job was done. "This will cure pretty good through the summer, and will burn real nicely when we need it next winter."

"Are we going to saw down any more trees, Dad?" Dan asked.

"One more," replied his father, grinning at his younger son. "Why? Getting tired?"

"Darn tired," said Dan.

They laughed, and Mr. Chekko ruffled the boy's hair. "It's the law of the game, Dan," he said sympathetically. "We've got to work to eat, work to keep warm. I'm going to buy a few tons of coal, too, but the more wood we burn, the more money we'll save."

That, Billy knew, was the crux of the whole thing. Keeping expenses down, and saving money. Mom and Dad sure didn't have it easy.

"Can I stay after school tomorrow and practice with the track team, Dad?" asked Billy. "I've missed two practices already."

"What's tomorrow? Thursday? Okay. You can practice. But if Dan and I are in the woods you'd better hightail it out there as soon as you get home."

"Okay." He knew he'd have to go out to help his father and Dan even if he was dead tired from practicing, but it was worth it. Running remained uppermost in his mind, and he didn't want to miss the opportunity to run on Cove Hill's track team.

As they headed for the house, Dan asked him if he knew that there was going to be a meet tomorrow between Cove Hill and Mercer.

"No," said Billy. He never discussed his running at home unless someone else mentioned the subject first.

He hadn't heard about it, nor had he paid any attention to the notices that were up on the bulletin board. Usually they were about careers, and he wasn't keenly interested in them yet.

"You going?" Dan asked.

Billy glared at him. "Sure I'm going!"

He hadn't seen Wendy all week, except from a distance that was often too far to speak across. But he would catch a light in her eyes that suggested to him that she had very much noticed him, and might even wish that he would make an effort to go to her and say something. But he didn't feel secure enough to talk to her. He felt sure that she was only singling him out because she was sorry for him, and he despised that.

She was at the meet with two other girls, one of

whom was the auburn-haired Pearl McCarthy. He didn't know the other one — a tall, skinny brunette — and didn't much care if he ever did.

He sensed Wendy looking at him as he trotted by her on his way to the other runners grouping around Coach Seavers.

"Hi," she said.

"Hi," he answered.

"Good luck!" she called to him.

"Thanks!"

He came to a stop in the rear of the ring that formed in front of the coach, but it was as if that mastermind had seen him approaching and was waiting for him.

"Chekko!"

"Yes, sir."

"What do you think this is, a social event that you can come to any time you wish? Where were you during the rest of the week?"

"I had to work, sir. Help my father."

"Okay. Fine. I can appreciate that. But I can't tolerate it." His boisterous voice carried even beyond the perimeter of listeners. It was evident he didn't care who else heard him. "Your father doesn't work on Fridays?"

"He works every day, sir. From seven to three. Except weekends." Billy's eyes went past the coach's, looked at nothing in particular. His lower lip quivered. The coach either enjoyed embarrassing him in front of all these people or else he didn't care.

"Okay, Chekko. I'm not going to ask you to go into detail for me about what kind of work you help your father with. I only hope it'll help in what *I* want you to do. Do I make myself clear, Chekko?"

"Yes, sir."

"Good. Okay, men," he said, turning his attention to the whole team now. "We're competing in a practice session with Mercer. They win a lot of meets, but we're not concerned about that today. We're only interested in competition. Who wins or loses makes no difference. But —" He paused to let the word sink into the athletes' minds — "that doesn't mean you're at liberty to run or jump or whatever with only two-thirds or even nine-tenths of your capabilities!" he went on, his voice rising. "I want you to put your one hundred percent into it! Understand? I want you to *think* it's the real thing! That you are here to win! And if you've got any other thoughts about that on your minds you're on the wrong team!"

Then he let his eyes rove over each and every man, as if to challenge them one by one. No one said a word.

Chapter 8

BILLY WATCHED the sixty and the one-hundred-yard dashes, both won easily by Cody Jones. He couldn't help noticing Pearl McCarthy rush up to Cody, throw her arms around his neck, and kiss him after each win, while Wendy and the other girl stood back and watched.

He didn't know what he was going to run in, but he hoped it would be the eight-eighty, the mile, and the two-mile, the distances he had signed up for. He felt certain that he could perform better in those distances than in any others.

What's the coach going to do? he wondered. Wait till the last minute before he tells me? Most of the other guys seemed to know in which races they were to run, but not him.

Well, he was sure he would've known if he'd been at the workouts every day. Maybe the coach kept him in suspense until the last minute to teach him a lesson.

"Okay, Chekko. Get ready for the two-twenty,"

Coach Seavers said, surprising him by coming up behind him and grabbing his elbow. "I want to see what you can do. Remember, pick up those knees. Pump those arms. Exert yourself the entire distance. Exert, exert, exert. Be ready, Chekko."

"Thanks, Coach."

The two-twenty? Oh, man.

From that moment on he began to feel like a bundle of wires, each one being stretched to the breaking point. He tried to avoid Wendy's eyes when she came near him. He didn't want her to see how nervous he was.

"Well, Billy, which one are you in, huh?" asked Cody, smiling with the confidence of a winner. "Or ain'tcha?"

"The two-twenty," replied Billy.

"So am I! How about that? Any other?"

"I don't know. The coach didn't say."

He warmed up for the race by jogging on the track with the other runners between races. Then the order came that the two-twenty was to start in two minutes, and the runners got ready. There were four, two from each school. *Me and Cody running for Cove Hill,* thought Billy. *Me, when the coach could have picked one or two others who surely must be faster than I am.*

7 1

The runners were given their lanes. Billy was in lane two. The runners on either side of him were from Mercer. Cody was in lane four.

They set their starting chocks in place. First the left, then the right, the left again till the runners were satisfied.

"Take your mark!" called the starter.

Billy crouched down, held his fingers tightly together and laid the tips down against the cindered track, his right knee down, his foot back.

"Get set!"

He lifted his knees, pushed his body slightly forward, got his drive leg — the left leg — ready to catapult him.

Bang! went the gun.

Billy took off, putting pressure against the chock with his left leg to give him the momentum he needed. Then he was up and away, arms pumping at his sides, legs pounding under him as fast as he could make them go.

Even before the runners had gone ten yards Billy saw the ones on either side of him moving slowly past him. He kept his eyes straight ahead, but from the corner of his right eye he could see Cody and the runner beside him out-distancing him by two yards . . . three yards . . . and steadily gaining.

He struggled hard to catch up, to make a better showing, but his legs just wouldn't produce. Then it was over. A Mercer runner won; Cody came in second. Billy, a pitiful last.

"Yay, Billy!" an unfamiliar voice shouted from the crowd. "You get the booby prize, Billy!"

Someone else yelled another humiliating remark at him, and he wanted to head for the locker room before there was a chorus of them. But he knew he couldn't do that. He had to stay, to face the humiliation, whether he was going to run in another race or not.

The runners kept running on the track, gradually slowing their paces as they turned around and came back.

Billy saw the coach approach and talk to Cody, who was bent over now, hands on his knees, still breathing heavily from the run. For a second their eyes met — Billy's and Coach Seaver's — and Billy wondered whether the coach might want to say something to him. Insult him. Criticize him. For it seemed that it was only to the best performers that he offered genuine praise.

But the coach's eyes shifted back to Cody as if they hadn't met Billy's at all. Billy looked away, and walked over to the area where the discus throwing meet was taking place. He stayed there till a girl, one of the scorekeepers, tapped him on the elbow and said that the coach wanted to see him.

"See me?" he echoed. "What does he want to see me about?"

"I think he wants you to run in the four-forty, too," she said.

He stared at her. "You sure?"

"Well, that's the next race coming up," she said. "I'm just guessing."

He ran back to the track where he saw Coach Seavers talking now to Luke Maynard and Dick Koski, a blond-haired youth about six inches shorter than Luke.

"You want me, Coach?"

"Yes, I do, Chekko. How do you feel?"

"Okay."

"Fine. I want to see what you can do in the four-forty."

"I'll try my best, sir."

"You tried your best in the two-twenty," said the coach tartly. "It wasn't very good."

"I know. I'm sorry."

"You sure you're not too tired?"

"I'm sure."

"Okay. You're running with Maynard and Koski." A whistle shrieked close by. "Get going. Give me all you've got. Okay?"

"Okay, Coach," all three of them said, almost in unison.

The race for first place was close. Mercer again took it, but it was only by a step. Each team had three runners competing. Koski came in second, Luke third. Billy came in next to last.

After a brief tapering-off run, he bent over and put his hands on his knees. Sweat poured off his face. His chest heaved. He felt disgraced, humiliated. Last, and then next to last. It wasn't much of an improvement.

"You okay, Chekko?" said a voice.

He shook his head. "I'm okay. Just winded."

The coach patted him on the back. "You slowed down in that last seventy to eighty yards," he said curtly. "I think that work you're doing at home tired you, Chekko. Better get a good rest tonight."

"Yes, sir."

Billy straightened up, and saw the coach walking toward the girl who had informed Billy earlier that the coach wanted to see him. He suddenly felt alone and ignored, but he hardly cared.

Dan and Christina came running up to him.

"You're not going home, are you?" Christina asked, looking at him intently.

"Yes, I am. Right after I shower."

"Can we stay?" asked Dan. "We'll go home on the spectators' bus."

Billy shrugged. "Okay by me."

"Thanks, Billy. See you later."

They ran off, and he turned and headed toward the school. Nice showing I made for you kids, wasn't it? he thought. Beats me why you want to stay. I'd think you'd be so ashamed of me you'd want to leave, too.

But why should they be ashamed of him? They were his family, but they were also individuals. They didn't necessarily have to suffer just because he did.

He had his gaze down, his mind wrapped up in thoughts, when a smooth, soft voice brought him out of his reverie.

"Billy? Penny for your thoughts."

He slowed his steps and turned. "Hi, Wendy."

"Where you going?"

"Home."

"You're not going to see the rest of the meet?"

"I've seen enough," he said.

He looked away from her and started on again.

"I thought you ran pretty well," she said. "You were ahead of all but one of them for over half the race. Did you know that?"

"No."

"Well, you were. Then you slowed down. Are you all right? I mean, do you feel okay?"

He nodded. "Just tired," he confessed.

There was a short pause. Neither one seemed to have any more to say.

"See you next week?" she said then.

"Sure."

While he was under the shower Wendy's words tumbled over and over again in his mind. *You were ahead of all but one of them for over half the race.* He remembered being ahead of two or three of the runners, but he hadn't realized he had led almost all of them that long. That definitely was an improvement over his performance in the first race. Perhaps the coach had figured it right. What slowed him down was the work — sawing, carrying, and chopping wood. But Billy saw no avenue of escape from those tasks. Mr. Chekko was as firm in having his sons help him with those muscle-straining chores as Coach Seavers was in building up a winning track team.

When he finished dressing he put his things, including the duffel bag, into his locker, and left. Why take the uniform home for a wash when it had hardly gotten soiled?

He started running the moment he got out the door. The shower had refreshed and relaxed him. He felt a mite tired, but figured that if he became too tired during the run he'd reduce his pace to a walk. The run home wasn't significant now. He just wanted to get away from the track. The sooner the better.

Twice he slowed his pace down to a walk. The school was four and a half miles from home. He had run the distance at least a dozen times. But the distance seemed longer now. He was tiring quicker than he could remember tiring before.

His mother stared at him as he entered the house. "I didn't hear the bus," she said.

"It hasn't come yet," he told her. "I ran home."

She looked into his eyes, searching his thoughts. "You didn't stay through the whole thing?"

"No."

"You lost, didn't you?"

"Yes. I was in two races, lost them both."

"And you got disgusted and came home."

"Yes."

He sat down by the kitchen window. Something was cooking in the oven. He sniffed but couldn't determine what it was.

"Why did you go out for track if you get disgusted so easily?" she asked him.

He was looking at the wall clock. It read ten to five. The meets usually got over between five and five-thirty.

"I thought I'd do better than I have," he confessed, turning his attention to his fingernails which, he saw, needed clipping.

"But you're just starting. What else can you expect? You want to be a champion right off the bat?"

He got up to look for the nail clippers. "I don't know what to expect," he said.

"Well, don't expect that," she said. "You have to creep first. It's like everything else a person wants to be a winner in. You have to start from the bottom of the totem pole."

"You're right, Mom," he said. "Way down on the bottom."

He found the clippers and stepped outside on the back porch to do the manicuring. He heard the splitting and thudding sound of wood being chopped, and saw his father busy wielding an axe by the woodpile.

"Hi, Dad!" he called.

"Hi, son!" replied his father.

"Need any help?"

"No! I'm almost finished!"

His father was a workhorse. How many men were there who'd come home from an eight-hour job and almost immediately start chopping wood? Weren't many, reflected Billy.

Fifteen minutes later the spectator bus hummed to

a stop in front of the house and deposited Dan and Christina. They came racing to the house, Dan beating his sister by two steps. Billy grinned as he watched them through the kitchen window.

Dan was first inside the house, his pace slowed down to a walk. Christina barged in, plowing into him and sending him crashing to the floor.

"What the heck's the matter with you?" he shouted, glaring up at her.

She stared at him, a hand to her mouth. "I'm sorry. I thought you were *way* inside."

"Dummy," he snorted, and got to his feet.

Billy put a hand over his mouth to cover a grin. Count on Dan to be involved in some kind of caper, whether planned or not.

"Mercer won," Christina announced, smiling now that she discovered Dan hadn't suffered any injuries.

"I thought no scores were kept," said Billy. "The coach said it was just a practice competition."

"Well, it was. But Jeannie kept score anyway. On her own."

"Jeannie?"

"The scorekeeper."

"Who won the mile?" asked Billy.

"Mercer. They won that and the two-mile."

"How come you weren't there?" asked his father,

his eyes riveted on Billy. "I thought you joined the track team."

"I did. I was in two races and lost."

"He finished last in one and next to last in the other," explained Dan soberly.

"He got discouraged with himself and came home," Christina chimed in, and looked at her older brother. "Maybe you should have stayed, Billy. Maybe Coach Seavers would've had you run in the relays. Or even the mile. That's where we really need some fast runners. We're weak as heck in those distances."

Billy met her brown eyes, saw them light up with enthusiasm. It was the first time she had looked so bright and healthy since she was sick, he thought.

"I think you're right, Chris," he said agreeably. "But it's up to the coach, not me." He shrugged. "I don't know. After I walked off like that, maybe he won't want me anymore."

Chapter 9

AFTER SUPPER Billy, Dan, and their father went into the woods again to saw down another tree and cut it to kindling size. The trunk of the pine tree Mr. Chekko selected this time was only slightly larger than those they had sawed down before, but the way Billy's arms began to feel as he pushed and pulled on the saw made him wonder if his father had found one six inches thicker.

At last Mr. Chekko's yell that they stop brought relief to Billy. He helped his father withdraw the saw from the tree, then watched him wield the axe till the tall pine fell exactly where he wanted it to.

A squirrel Billy hadn't seen on the tree before chittered with fright as it leaped through the air to another tree, landing on a slender branch that bounced up and down under its slight weight. Two crows screeched from the top of another tree and flew off; a rabbit skittered out from under a bush and ran madly until it vanished under another bush.

Again Billy and Dan sawed while their father

chopped, and it was twilight by the time the chunks were short enough to be carried to their back yard.

By now Billy was really tired. His arms felt ready to break off from his aching shoulders. His knees felt ready to collapse. His stomach was beginning to feel nauseous.

Suddenly his head became woozy, and he was afraid he was going to faint. "Watch it, Dan," he warned his brother, who was walking behind him.

He stopped and let the short log roll off his shoulder onto the ground, then he stepped off the path and lay down on the cool grass. He closed his eyes, while a myriad of tiny stars flashed before him.

He heard a second loud thud, and knew that Dan had dropped his log, too. "Billy! What's the matter? What happened?"

"I got dizzy," Billy murmured. His face was pale, his lips purple and dry.

"Shall I call Dad?"

"No. Let's wait a minute."

He waited there for a few minutes, until the wooziness was gone. Then he rose, lifted the log back up on his shoulder, and walked on.

"You sure you're okay now?" asked Dan worriedly.

"I'm sure," said Billy.

But he wasn't entirely okay. After he dropped the log off at home he told Dan that maybe he should tell their dad that he was sick, and that he was going into the house to lie down. Sheri, watching her brothers ever since they had come into sight from the woods, rushed into the house immediately to tell their mother that Billy was sick and "was coming in to lie down."

His mother was waiting for him when he reached the living room door. Not asking him a single question, she helped him to the sofa, then got a blanket with which she covered him.

"Did you throw up?" she asked him worriedly.

"No," he said.

She tucked the blanket under him. "I'm not surprised this happened," she said. "You've been working hard, and running hard. It's bound to get you eventually."

Later, after Billy had been in bed for about ten minutes, a knock sounded on the door and his father stepped into the room.

"You awake, son?" he whispered.

Billy opened his eyes. He was tired, but he hadn't fallen asleep yet. "Hi, Dad," he said.

"I'd like to talk to you a minute."

"Sure."

He came over, sat on the bed. A bristle of heavy beard had begun to show, and his shirt was open at the throat.

"I've been working you boys pretty hard," he admitted. "It's no easy job cutting down trees, turning them into firewood. But it's got to be done. And I can't do it all by myself. I need you boys to help me."

"I understand, Dad," said Billy, smiling.

He felt a hundred percent better than he did an hour ago. The nauseous sensation had left his stomach. His mind was clear. He just felt tired, and he was sure that a good night's rest would take care of that.

"Maybe you do," said Mr. Chekko, finding his son's warm arm under the blanket and rubbing it gently. "And maybe you don't. I know you like to run on your track team, and that perhaps it's because of the hard work I've put you to that you came in last and next to last in the races. But you must recognize priorities, Billy. In this case we're working together for the good of our family. We're fortunate that the wood is provided free to us. All we have to do is cut it down and reduce it to a usable size. And with the price of gas, coal, and electricity nowadays every bit of the work is worth it. You see what I'm driving at, Billy?"

Billy nodded. "There will be just the chopping

left to do," his father went on. "And I can do most of that. You helped me a lot. You and Dan both. I appreciate that. You're two of the best sons a father could be proud to have." He stood up, letting go Billy's arm. "Sleep tight. And don't think I'm far in left field when it comes to your running. I've read articles in the papers about it. I know how important it must be to you. Oh, one final thing before I leave you. Remember what I promised a little while back?"

Billy tried to remember, and a grin spread over his face. "About getting a car?"

"Right. I'm going to buy one this Saturday. How about that?"

"That'll be great, Dad!"

"I thought you'd like that. Good night, now. Sweet dreams."

"Good night, Dad."

The next day, Friday, seemed to be the culmination of all the bad things that happened during the week. Mr. Roche gave the math class a test that, Billy realized, was on a chapter he hadn't had time to study thoroughly. Math wasn't one of his favorite subjects anyway, which amplified his chances of scoring very poorly in it.

That day's French test might just result in a passing grade if Mrs. Tarkington had her heart in the right place, which she usually didn't. Billy didn't think he'd ever learn to understand her. He understood the French language better than he did her. Sometimes she'd mark off a point or two for misspelled words; sometimes she didn't. What she always did do was write her remarks in the margins in French. Sometimes they were clearly legible, and sometimes they weren't. It had become a game trying to translate a phrase he couldn't read.

He was glad that a weekend was coming between today and the next time he had to face Mr. Roche and Mrs. Tarkington. The grades he expected to receive from them weren't going to be ones he'd care to write his grandmother about (not that he would brag to her even if they turned out to be very good).

Seattle, Luke, and some of the other guys in the classes encountered him in the hall and asked him how he thought he had fared.

"Pas si bon," he answered.

He headed for his next class, and ran into Wendy. She looked radiant in a pink skirt and white blouse with sheer, flaring sleeves.

"Billy!" she exclaimed, stopping in front of him.

"Oh, hi," he said, smiling back at her. "How you doing?"

"Okay. What did you think of the math test?"

87

"I want to forget it."

"You don't think you'll pass it?"

"I'm sure I won't. I didn't go over the chapter. Didn't have time." He noticed the umbrella pendant she was wearing. "Hey, that's cute."

"Protection when I'm caught out in the rain," she said, beaming.

An awkward few seconds passed. Then she said, "You going to be at practice this afternoon?"

"I think I'd better, if I expect to stay on the squad," he confessed. "I'm barely hanging in there." The bell rang. "There she blows. See you later."

"At the track," she replied, and went past him, flashing that warm, beautiful smile that matched the brilliance of her pendant.

He turned and watched her for a minute, mentally cursing the bell for cutting their conversation short. So what if all they had talked about was trivia? It kept them together, that's what mattered.

For a minute, after he turned back and headed for his next class, he had to reorganize his thoughts to remember just which one he was going to.

"Destination Cove Hill Park. Run all the way to it, walk halfway around it, then break into a sprint and head for the Ludlow Rod and Gun Club." Coach Seavers's rapid-fire order had the attention of every member of the track team, including Billy, who felt good that the coach hadn't chewed him out for taking off before the meet was over yesterday. But there was still time for that. "When you get there, come back, alternating with walks, slow runs, and sprints. Seattle Williams will give you the orders. Everybody understand that?"

Nodding heads and a few muttered yeses gave evidence that everyone did. The group was comprised of only the runners; those involved in the sprints, hurdles, relays, and the longer distances. The discus throwers, high jumpers, broad jumpers, pole vaulters, and shot putters — members of the field events — had their own program, most of which was under the guidance of the assistant coach, Dick Rafini. The girls' track and field teams were grouped separately at the opposite end of the field.

"Okay. Take off!" commanded the coach.

The distance to Cove Hill Park was about a mile and a half. Around it was another two-thirds of a mile or so; no one had ever really measured it. From there to the Ludlow Rod and Gun Club, which was located on Salmon Creek, was about two miles. From the gun club back to the school was a mile and a half. So the total round-trip distance was slightly over five and a half miles.

Billy found himself running among the trailing

half of the crowd by the time they reached the park. He wasn't exerting himself, just dropping one foot after the other in a smooth, rhythmical pace.

During the sprints he noticed runners zipping past him. There weren't many because the fastest runners were far in the lead anyway. Seattle, Rudy, and Luke were practically in a category by themselves. A kid named Chuck Schwinn was close behind.

Seattle's loud yell, "Okay, walk!" seemed to come as a welcome relief to most of them, but Billy found that his running pace was comfortable enough that he could run on and on without getting more tired. But the sprints affected him, wore him down, so that by the time the twenty-two-man team was returning from the Rod and Gun Club he was beginning to feel the strain in his thighs and calves.

He discovered something else that gave him a lift. He was one of the first six to finish the practice run. Seattle had come in about fifty yards ahead of him, definitely the fastest of the squad. Luke was second, about twenty yards behind him, and Rudy only a few yards behind Luke. Two other runners filled the spread between Rudy and Billy. Even though the run was just a body, lung, and leg conditioner, Billy knew that most of the guys tried to make an impressive showing.

At the field there was a ten-minute rest period

during which the squad dropped like bundles of wet hay right on the spot where they were standing, when Coach Seavers announced the order. The cool grass was the next best thing to a shower.

Then came the loud, familiar bark again. "Okay, men! Up on your feet! Line up!"

A chorus of "Oh, no!" came on the heels of the order as the twenty-two athletes got slowly to their feet.

"Come on, you guys! You act as if you're half dead! Let's go! One! Two! One! Two!"

By the time the ten minutes of calisthenics were up, only Billy's dim awareness of what was going on around him made him certain he was more alive than dead.

Chapter 10

ON SATURDAY Buck Saunders, a neighbor, drove Mr. Chekko, Billy, and Dan to Lonsdale, dropped them off at a used car lot, and said he'd pick them up in two hours. Billy didn't care what kind of a car his father was going to buy. Anything would do as long as it ran. But he knew his father had his mind set on a Buick. He had always had a Buick and had been satisfied with it; his philosophy was, Why bother with a different make of car if you're not sure how it's going to perform?

They covered three lots before Mr. Chekko found a car he liked and could afford to buy. It was a cream-colored four-door sedan with vinyl seats, AM–FM radio, and even a mounted compass on the snazzy-looking dashboard.

Billy couldn't get over how simple the whole business was. The salesman handled the entire transaction, even down to getting the information to the insurance company of Mr. Chekko's own choice. Mr. Chekko made a down payment by check, was given a coupon book, and told that the car would be delivered directly to his home the following Wednesday.

The thrill of finally having a car in the family left Billy in a stupor. He couldn't believe that his father had really gone and done it. Billy thought that the moment the deal was over he would let out a yell, make some kind of noise to celebrate the event. But he didn't feel like doing anything like that. Dan didn't seem to feel like it either, as if he too were in a state of shock.

Only their father was outwardly affected. He was whistling.

It wasn't till Buck Saunders picked them up that both Billy and Dan opened up, exuding excitement and joy about their new car. It was three years old, but to them it was like brand new.

"We rode in it," Billy declared from the back seat. "It rides like a boat. Real smooth. Wow!"

"The radio works great," added Dan. "We got a dozen stations, all clear as a bell. Right, Billy?"

"Right."

Their father didn't have much of an opportunity to put in his two cents worth, but his happy smile was enough to express the joy that he was feeling. Both Mr. Chekko and Billy studied the driver's manual that the car salesman had given them, so that by the time the car was delivered they'd know all about driving.

Billy really hoped he'd learn to drive the car. He wasn't old enough to take a driver's test, but he could see no harm in learning how to drive a car now so that by the time he was sixteen and had a junior operator's license he'd be an expert.

Having a car would eliminate the trips on foot to New Court and back — for groceries, for drugs, for anything that his mother thought the family needed. Running was fun. But combining it with carrying groceries turned it into a wretched task. Most of the time he did the errands willingly, but he wished such tasks weren't necessary. Now that he was in track he didn't need an extracurricular activity to get in shape.

The weekend sped by. On Monday he stayed after school for track practice, wondering if he was improving. When he felt a sharp burn on the back of his right heel and removed his shoes, he saw that a blister had formed and torn open. He got a Band-Aid from the manager and applied it to the sore, hoping it would heal before the next meet, which was on Friday.

After supper that night Buck Saunders came over to teach the rudiments of driving to Mr. Chekko, who had picked up a three months' driving permit during his lunch hour. It was more of a refresher course, since Mr. Chekko had driven before. Billy could hardly wait till his father was again familiar enough with the shifting, braking, and steering to instruct him.

On Tuesday Billy learned that the math test he had taken last Friday had proved to be a disaster, which didn't surprise him one bit. He got a 48. Mrs. Tarkington gave him a grade of 76 on his French test, which was just one point over the passing mark. It was better than he expected.

On Wednesday, the day the Buick was to be delivered, Billy was called to the office of the vice principal, Mr. Keating, who looked like a kindly man, with dark-rimmed glasses and a perpetual smile, but wasn't. Billy didn't think he had ever seen a more deceptive face in his life.

"I thought I had better talk to you personally, William," Mr. Keating said in a level voice, eyeing Billy with a soft, froggish stare. "Your grades have indicated a decrease in effort over the last few weeks, particularly in math. That mark of forty-eight that you received in last Friday's test is atrocious. Your grades in social studies and history are only slightly better. I've got to have a promise from you, William, that you're going to make an honest effort to up your grades or, I'm afraid, your days as a trackman will be over."

The tone of his voice hardly changed throughout his monologue, but Billy got the point.

"I'm sorry. I promise I'll do better, sir."

"Or you're off the track team," Mr. Keating reminded him. "Remember that."

"I will."

Billy started to put more time into his studies that very night. He had an ambition to be a trackman; he had no intention of letting it be taken away from him.

Coach Seavers had the trackmen repeat the run-walk-and-sprint routine down to Cove Hill Park and the Rod and Gun Club on Thursday. It was while they were on their way back to the school that Billy felt the sore on the back of his heel again.

Oh, no! he thought despairingly. Not again! He had practically forgotten about it.

He stopped, removed his shoe and sock and saw that the Band-Aid had slipped off the sore blister. He put it back on, but the gummed part of the Band-Aid was nearly dry and he doubted it would stay.

It didn't, as he discovered after he had run awhile and began to feel the soreness again. For most of the remaining half a mile or so he hobbled, and was one of the last to arrive at the track, where Coach Seavers was standing with Coach Rafini, waiting for them.

"What happened to you, Chekko?" Coach Seavers snapped.

"Got a blister on my left heel," said Billy.

"See Mary," he ordered. "Have her put a Band-Aid on it. And you'd better get a new pair of shoes."

Billy didn't tell him that the blister had happened Monday. Nodding, he went over to the manager, took off his shoes and socks, and had her give him another Band-Aid.

On Friday he had a test again in math, and he thought he did well on it.

He also had tests in French and social studies, and was confident he did well on them, too. But he remained in suspense till the sound of the final bell, wondering if one of his teachers, or Mr. Keating, was going to draw him aside and tell him his grades hadn't been raised high enough to justify his suiting up for the track meet that afternoon. But no one called him.

The voice he did hear calling his name in the hall belonged to Wendy. "Billy! Oh, Billy! Can I see you a minute?"

He turned, and let his smile answer for him.

She came running toward him, a small stack of books cradled in her arms.

"Hear anything about the tests?" she asked.

"Nope. Which is good news, because as long as I don't, I can still be on the track squad." He grabbed her wrist and looked at her wristwatch. "I'm sorry, Wendy. I've got to go. Coach wants us at the track by three-fifteen."

"I'll be there, too," she said, smiling. "As a spectator, of course."

"Good. I'll see you."

He hurried to the locker room and found nearly the entire team already there, suiting up. When he was ready he ran out, testing the blistered heel as he pumped his legs high but slowly. He barely felt the sore, and wasn't worried that it would bother him.

He jogged all the way to the track, and was almost within arm's distance of his sister and brother, who were standing among other students their age, before he saw them.

"Hi, Dan. Hi, Chris," he said.

They answered him, smiles of hope and encouragement on their faces. But they said nothing more and he ran on to the track where the rest of the runners were assembling around the coaches, Seavers and Rafini.

The meet was the league's first of the season. Competing with Cove Hill was Bentley-Hall. Billy didn't know how strong they were, nor did he care. His main concern was to run, and he waited hopefully for one of the coaches to tell him in which races he was to participate.

Soon there was action at the discus-throwing section, the broad jump, the high jump. Billy watched the one-hundred-yard dash, and felt tension ignite as a Bentley-Hall runner kept up a neck-to-neck stride with Cody Jones. All the other runners trailed those two by at least a dozen steps, and failed to threaten. But this was the first time that Billy had seen anyone matching Cody in the one-hundred-yard sprint, and the tension mounted till the very moment they crossed the finish line.

A cheer exploded from the Bentley-Hall fans as their hero flashed across the tape a step ahead of Cody. The Cove Hill fans seemed stunned. They hadn't expected this. No one had beaten Cody in the one-hundred and two-hundred-twenty-yard dashes in two years.

The fear hung over the heads of the Cove Hill squad and fans that maybe the Bentley-Hall winner would take the two-twenty also. Maybe even the four-forty. He was a tall kid, about six feet, with a strong, well-muscled body that indicated many days of training and exercise. He looked formidable, a threat to any opponent. Billy wished he could run against him. Not now, but sometime in the future.

He found himself near Coach Seavers, and wanted

desperately to go up closer to him and ask him in which race he was going to run. But the coach seemed busy talking strategy with his assistant.

Seattle and Rudy then cornered him about something that seemed important to them. Dave Colloni, the two-hundred-pound discus-thrower, came forward and talked with the coach for five minutes, then left, a smile of encouragement on his face.

By now Billy's desire to talk to the coach had dissipated. The heck, he thought. He sees me here. He'll tell me if he wants to.

The two-hundred-twenty-yard race was soon to begin. Cody and Rudy were the two chosen to run in it.

Billy watched the race from some twenty feet behind the spectators lined up at the rope. Each school had two runners entered. Each had fans sitting in the small grandstand ready to lead them in victory yells that were supposed to psych up their teams.

At the gun the runners took off. Billy's eyes were on Cody from the instant the gun fired, then they shifted to Rudy, who, running even with Cody for about twenty yards, began to fall back. He turned his attention to the tall Bentley-Hall kid, and saw him streaking ahead of the bunch. Then Cody crept up, inching forward slowly as the yards flashed by under his feet.

As the two runners raced across the finish line a yell broke from a handful of spectators who were standing in line with it and were able to see who had won. Billy saw Cody swing up his arms in victory, and heard the victory cheer come from the Cove Hill fans in the grandstand.

Even though Billy placed Cody near the bottom of his friendship totem pole, he still felt a flash of excitement for Cody's win. Beating that tall kid from Bentley-Hall was something. Cody deserved a lot of credit.

But where will I come in? Billy thought. Or won't I even get the chance?

Chapter 11

THE TWO-HUNDRED-YARD HURDLES were next. On other parts of the field the pole vault, the running broad jump, the high jump, and the discus events were taking place in their scheduled order, but Billy had no interest in them. He didn't really care about the hurdles, either; he only stayed because he wanted to keep Coach Seavers in his sight.

The gun went off for the two-hundred-yard hurdle race, and Jim Morris, running for Cove Hill, took the lead immediately. He held it for about half the distance, then began to give ground to Bentley-Hall and finished second.

Billy saw the girl with the scorebook running by him and called to her.

"Mary! When's the four-forty?" he asked her.

"After the medley relay," she said. "That comes up next."

"Am I in it, do you know?"

She glanced at the scorebook, then back at him. "The four-forty? I don't know, Billy. You'll have to ask Coach Seavers. Sorry, I've got to go."

"Will — will *you* ask him?"

Her eyes appraised him. "Okay."

"Thanks."

When she came back a few minutes later the look in her eyes offered him no encouragement.

"Did you ask him?" Billy inquired.

"Yes."

"What did he say?"

"He wouldn't tell me."

Billy stared at her. "He wouldn't tell you?"

"No. Sorry, Billy."

A mixture of hurt and anger took hold in his stomach. Why didn't the coach tell him in which race he was going to run? Why was he being ignored? If I hadn't been coming to the practices the last few times, I'd understand it, Billy thought. And if my marks were below passing I'd understand it, too. But I've attended the practices, and my marks are up. What's he got against me?

"Hi," said a voice beside him.

It startled him, even though it was soft and familiar.

"Hi, Wendy," he said. "Where you been?"

"I had to go home. Dental appointment. Are you going to be in the four-forty?"

"I don't know. I don't know *what* I'm going to be in."

They watched the medley relay. Each school had a runner in the four-forty, the two consecutive two-twenties, and the eight-eighty, all of which made up the relay. Cody was the representative runner in this final distance, and came through the winner, conquering a five-yard deficit he had to start with.

It looked like Rudy and Chuck Schwinn were the coach's choices for the four-forty. Billy, gazing in the direction of the starting line, saw the two runners assembling there with Coach Seavers. The Bentley-Hall runners and their coach were also getting together in the area. Rudy and Chuck were hopping up and down, getting their blood stimulated for the run.

"Maybe he'll have you run in the mile," Wendy surmised.

"It seems he would have told me," said Billy.

In a few minutes the runners lined up for the four-hundred-and-forty-yard race. Billy put his money on Chuck, although there was a six-footer running for Bentley-Hall who was probably the strongest competitor ever to come up against the Cove Hill runner.

The gun went off and the tall Bentley-Hall runner took the lead. Halfway through the distance Chuck crept past him and moved into first place. He retained the lead for the next fifty yards. Then Bentley-Hall seemed to open up stored power and quickly closed the gap between him and Chuck. For a few seconds they were neck and neck. Then, with ten yards to go, he seemed to hurl past Chuck and won by two steps.

"The guy runs like a greyhound," said Billy.

"I'll say," Wendy agreed.

He saw the coach moving away from the track, scratching his head. Billy ran over to him.

"Coach Seavers," he said.

He went on impulsively now. He had to, or he might change his mind.

The coach looked up at him. "What do you want, Chekko?"

"Am I going to run?"

"With a blistered heel? You out of your mind? No, you're not going to run."

He started to go on. Billy ran in front of him. "But my heel's okay, Coach! It's not bothering me! I can run!"

The coach looked at him. "Chekko, do I have to drill it into your head? You're not *there* yet. You can't deliver. I'm choosing the guys that are more apt to deliver, Chekko. Sorry, but you asked for it, Chekko. Now out of my way. I've got work to do."

He brushed Billy out of his way and marched across the field, his stride exceptionally long for a man of his size. Billy watched him, resentment festering inside him.

Can't deliver? Baloney!

Wendy came up beside him. "What did he say?"

"First he said he's not having me run because of the blister on my heel. Then he tells me what he really thinks. That I'm not *there* yet. That I can't deliver."

"He's got too much on his mind," said Wendy.

"Oh, sure. Too much on his mind. Baloney. I've got a good notion to turn in my uniform and tell him what he can do with it," said Billy hotly, staring into the crowd for the coach's broad back, but not seeing it anymore.

Wendy grabbed his hand. "Don't," she said. "Do as he says. Take care of that heel, and then run and run and run. Because you *can* run, Billy. And I think he knows it. He just wants you to get better. He's tough, but he's honest."

"You believe all that?"

"Yes, I do."

He shrugged. "Well, maybe you're right. But I'd forgotten about my heel."

"It isn't sore?"

"No. I suppose it might get sore if I ran any distance, like the eight-eighty or the mile." He sighed. "I'd better get a new pair of track shoes. I want to run. I want to prove to Coach Seavers I can run."

Wendy smiled.

"Can I change the subject for a minute?"

"Sure."

"There's a movie at the school a week from Saturday night. You going to it?"

"I hadn't thought about it," he confessed.

"Would you think about it?" she asked. "And would you think about taking me with you?" She laughed, and looked away from him when he met her eyes. "I'm sorry. Maybe you wouldn't want to take me. What I said came out without my thinking. I'll go. I'll see you later."

She started to turn away, and he grabbed her arm. "No. Wait a minute. Who said I wouldn't want to take you? I'd rather take you than any other girl in school."

"You sure?"

"Yes, I'm sure. What time's the movie?"

"Eight."

"Okay. I'll see you about twenty of."

"How? I know you haven't got a car."

"My father bought one last week. He's learning to drive it. He's only got a permit, but maybe he can get someone to ride with him who has a license. He's got some friends."

"But my father can drive us," she said. "He won't mind. Now don't argue. Please," she said, when he started to interrupt. "I know it'll be all right."

"Okay." He felt as light as a feather. He could run the eight-eighty and win it by ten yards, sore heel or not.

They watched the mile race together, which was won by Bentley-Hall. Cove Hill, represented by Dick Koski, came in second.

Dick also came in second in the two-mile race. Winning it by a wide margin was the same kid who had won the mile.

Later, the ride home on the bus turned out to be more embarrassing than Billy expected. The other riders were all ears as Dan and Christina asked Billy why he hadn't run in any of the races.

He didn't know what to tell them except the truth. "Coach didn't ask me."

Chapter 12

A CLOUDLESS SKY on Saturday morning gave promise of a bright, clear day, and Billy's father took advantage of it to improve his driving skills. His training ground was a road that ran at a right angle to their road. There was hardly any traffic on it, and chances were remote that a cop would be driving on it.

He practiced parking on a grade as well as on the level, making turns in the road, braking without jolting the car, and starting off from a dead stop with ease and smoothness. His dad was doing so well that Billy was sure he could pass a driver's test without trouble.

"In another week," said Mr. Chekko.

"Will you teach me now, Dad?" asked Billy anxiously.

Mr. Chekko stared at him. "Teach you? What are you talking about, Billy? You're only fourteen. You won't be old enough to drive for another three years yet. Two years, if you get your junior's license when you're sixteen."

Billy's heart flipped. He looked at his father, shocked by his answer. Ever since the family had purchased the car Billy had expected to learn to drive it, too. There had never been the slightest suspicion in his mind that his father would object to it. Now the reply left him cold and heartsick.

"But I thought you'd let me, Dad," murmured Billy. "I thought all along —"

"Well, you thought wrong, Billy," his father interrupted. "There's no sense at all for you to learn how to drive a car now, so just forget about it. Don't worry, when the time comes I'll teach you."

If that final remark was supposed to make Billy feel better, it didn't. And the excitement that had consumed Billy when the car was purchased drained from him. Right now he didn't care if they had a car or not.

Billy bought a new pair of track shoes on Saturday. He made sure they fit.

On Monday, Cody and Rudy cornered him as he was heading for his first class.

"You didn't run at all on Friday," said Cody, a glint of mockery in his eyes. "How come?"

"Coach didn't ask me to."

"Somebody said that you didn't want to run because of a blister on your foot," Rudy interposed.

"It was on my heel," said Billy, making it specific. He didn't go into further detail about what the coach had said.

Cody glanced at Rudy. "A blistered heel? Sounds like an excuse. What's your analysis, Rudy?"

"Well, I can't say that Billy has been a threatening competitor, can you?"

"No, I can't. So his not running in any of the races last Friday could only mean one thing. Right?"

"Right. He was afraid he'd end up tailend Charlie, just like he did in the practice meets against Mercer."

Billy, his temper touched off by the guys' teasing remarks, started to turn and head up the hall when he realized that a small throng had already formed around them. Their sly, amused looks as they focused their attention on him made his face turn hot with embarrassment. He was in the thick of it now; Cody and Rudy had cleverly woven him into their web.

Cody took notice of the group around them, and he chuckled with amusement. "You're pretty popular, Billy. Look at your admirers. I'd sure feel like bursting with pride if I were you."

Billy met his eyes squarely. "I'm going to make you eat every one of your words one of these days, Cody," he said stiffly. "Not one of these days. *Today.*"

"You are?" Cody laughed. "When? And how?"

"By challenging you to a race, that's how."

Rudy stared at him. "You must be crazy, man."

A chuckle rippled from someone in the audience.

"Any distance. You name it," said Billy.

He spoke quickly, without weighing what he said. He had been humiliated enough by Cody, and he was promising himself that he wasn't going to let the damn guy get away with it again.

"Any distance? You know I can take you in the hundred. Easily."

"I said you name it," repeated Billy, tight-lipped.

Suddenly Cody seemed a trifle uncomfortable. "How about making a bet first?"

"Okay. But keep it under a dollar."

"I'm not thinking of money," said Cody. "I'm thinking of something more interesting."

"Like what?"

"Like the winner takes Wendy to the movie Saturday night."

Billy caught his breath and stared at Cody. Laughter sprang from the small throng.

"Take him up on it, Billy," someone remarked.

"Sure. Don't be chicken," said another.

Cody's bet ricocheted in Billy's mind. "She's going with me," he said.

"I heard she was. But if I win, she goes with me."

"Take him up on it, Billy," another voice broke in from the group.

"Quiet," said Rudy. "Let him make up his own mind."

"You heard me," said Cody. "Take it or leave it."

Billy licked his dry lips. *You rat,* he thought. "Okay." The word sounded as if it had come from someone else.

"Thanks." Cody smiled. "We'll run the hundred."

"Boooo!" exploded from the group.

"Give him a break! Make it the four-forty!" one kid shouted.

That there was at least one kid siding with him salved Billy's feelings. But it wasn't much help.

Cody's face reddened. "Okay. We'll run the four-forty," he said.

"Okay. The four-forty," Billy agreed.

"Name the time and place," said Cody.

"This noon," replied Billy. "At the track."

"You're on."

They shook hands on it.

A gang of about seventy-five students were at the track during lunch hour, waiting anxiously for the race to begin.

Billy had succeeded in avoiding Wendy all morning, and hoped she hadn't heard about this. So her reaction to the race was still to come. He dreaded to see the moment.

He realized later how crazy he was for having agreed with Cody on the bet. Cody had caught him off guard, hadn't given him enough time to consider it. It was foolish, ridiculous. Wendy was not a *thing*. She wasn't a slave. She couldn't be placed on a pedestal and bet on.

But that was what Cody and he had done. Placed her on a pedestal and bet on her. And now that the bet was on, Billy was committed. But, because the race was the four-forty, Billy felt he had a chance. A slim chance.

They both carried their track shoes to the track, and put them on. A kid was selected to start them off at the starting line. Rudy volunteered to be the judge at the finish line. There was no other change in the runner's dress. They both wore the same clothes they had worn to school.

"You ready to go?" asked Seattle.

"I'm ready," agreed Billy.

They stepped on the track and got in position at the starting line.

"On your mark! Get set! Go!" shouted the starter.

The runners took off. Billy tried to get the jump on Cody, but knew the instant they started that he hadn't. He ran hard, pumping his arms, legs, gritting his teeth.

At about the halfway mark he inched up to Cody's side, and went past him by half a step. But at about the three-quarter mark he saw, from the corner of his eye, Cody again creeping up, and gradually gaining on him.

Billy tried to get his legs to move faster, to make a last ditch effort to forge ahead. But he lacked the stamina. When they crossed the finish line Cody was only a step ahead of him. But a step was all he needed.

A cheer went up from the onlookers. Rudy and several of Cody's friends rushed to him and showered the winner with plaudits. A few of the students came over to Billy and offered their condolences.

He turned, started to head back to the school, and found himself staring into an aggrieved face. His heart felt as if it had been pierced by an arrow.

"Did you — hear about the bet?" he said.

Tears blurred Wendy's eyes. "You dare to speak to me after that? Yes, I heard about it. Who hasn't? What do you think I am? I wouldn't ever go to a movie with him, or you either, Billy Chekko! I hate you! I don't ever want to see you again!"

She turned and fled toward the school, her dress flying up behind her, her words echoing and re-echoing in his mind as Billy stared helplessly after her. It was a wonder she hadn't slapped his face; he felt that he deserved that, too.

He returned to the school, despising himself for challenging Cody to a race, despising Cody for making that utterly ridiculous bet, and despising himself for agreeing to it. That foolish agreement had ruined the finest friendship he had ever had.

He was in the library during study hall, researching material for social studies, when he saw Wendy come in. Barely looking around her, she headed for one of the shelves of books, selected a volume, and carried it to a table. She was glancing at it when Billy came up quietly beside her.

"Wendy," he said softly. "I've got to talk to you."

She looked at him, and her eyes blinked. "I told you I don't want to speak to you anymore!" she said bitterly. "Go away!"

"Wendy, please."

"No!" She picked up her book and moved angrily to another table.

Billy felt eyes upon him, and blushed with embarrassment as he saw half a dozen or so other students in the room staring at him and Wendy. He went back to the table he had been sitting at and stared down at the book before him, looking at the words but not seeing them.

He wished he were dead.

Chapter 13

"*THERE WAS* more blasting today," said Billy's mother, sitting in the living room with a partially finished woolen rug sprawled across her lap. She had started to hook it last week, hoping to get it done by Christina's birthday. "We all went up in the field again, except Mrs. Shuler. She fell and hurt her hip the other day, and you couldn't get her out with a forklift."

"You'd need more than a forklift," said her husband, looking over the morning paper. "She must weigh three hundred if she weighs an ounce."

"When's supper going to be ready, Mom?" asked Billy.

He was lying on the floor, one leg cocked over the other, hands crossed over his head. The day had been the worst he had lived through in a long time, and he didn't want to lie here any longer thinking about it. No matter how he tried to think of something else, Wendy's angry face and bitter words were too strong to blot out.

"The usual time," said his mother. "Six o'clock."

Suddenly he wished he hadn't asked. He had thought about asking his father if the two of them could drive over to Ulster Road and practice, but he just remembered what his father had told him about learning to drive. Why go out in the car if he couldn't drive it, too? Forget it.

"Why'd you want to know?" His father's voice sliced into his thoughts.

Billy shrugged. "Oh, nothing important."

"Want something to do to kill some time?"

Billy heard the rustle of the newspaper as his father folded it and pushed it into an already jammed magazine rack.

"Not necessarily."

From the corner of his eye Billy saw his father rise from his chair.

"Come on," said his father. "We've got about half an hour."

Billy looked at him, hope brightening his eyes. "We?"

His father grimaced. "Look, Billy, I told you that you've still got three years to go yet before you can learn to drive a car," he said stolidly. "That's final. But that doesn't mean you can't come along and sit beside me in the car and watch how I do it."

The hope perished.

"I'd rather stay here."

"Billy!" exclaimed his mother. "What's got into you, anyway?"

"He's sore because I laid it on the line to him that I don't want him learning to drive a car till he's old enough to get a junior driver's license," Mr. Chekko explained placidly. "At fourteen he's too young. He'll just be tempted to get in the car and go somewhere, even if it's just down to the end of this road. If he happened to be caught by a cruising cop it'd be my tail."

"Your father's right, Billy," said his mother. "I'm surprised that you should act like a two-year-old about it. Why don't you go with your father? Maybe he needs your moral support."

He wanted to hear no more of it, so he got up and went to the closet for his jacket. He followed his father out of the house and to the car parked in the driveway beside it.

"I haven't heard you say anything lately about track," said his father as he backed the car out to the road. He didn't seem to have any trouble backing up, Billy observed.

"That's because I haven't been too involved," he said. "I didn't run at all last Friday."

Mr. Chekko shifted the lever into Drive, and the car shot ahead. "Why not?"

"Because of a blister I had on the back of my heel, something that the coach thought should heal real well before I run again," answered Billy. "And because he doesn't think I'm fast enough to compete."

"Maybe he's right."

"I don't know. Maybe he is. But now I feel sure I can do better in the mile and two-mile races. I'm more used to the long-distance runs."

"Have you told him that?"

"No."

"Maybe you should."

"I'm not going to tell him anything," said Billy. "Not anymore."

His dad drove to Ulster Road, made the left turn and drove up it, going slightly faster than he usually did. A truck came hurtling toward them. Quickly Mr. Chekko turned the wheel, pulling the car toward the side of the road.

"The crazy nut!" he exclaimed.

As the truck whizzed by, the car started to slide off the shoulder into a ditch. His father cursed as he turned the wheel fiercely to the left and stepped on the accelerator at the same time.

But, instead of veering back onto the road, the car slipped farther into the ditch. His father removed his foot from the accelerator and hit the brakes, but by then the car had struck the bank with a severe crunch. Billy's dad careened against the steering wheel and Billy against the dash, their seatbelts cushioning the shock.

Father and son stared at each other. "You okay?" asked Billy's father, his chest heaving.

"Yes. How about you?" Billy was shaken up, but not hurt.

"I'm all right."

His father shifted the gear lever into reverse and gunned the motor. The car backed up about a foot and lodged there, the motor racing, right wheel spinning.

"I think we're in solid, Dad," surmised Billy.

"You think? I know!" said Mr. Chekko, shutting off the engine. "Of all the luck. If the front end's damaged I'll have to postpone taking my driving test. I was hoping to make an appointment week after next."

He and Billy unbuckled their seatbelts and got out of the car. They stepped into the ditch and took inventory of the damage done.

"Well, the right fender and the bumper are bent," Mr. Chekko observed, disappointment in his voice. "Bad enough, but it could've been worse."

They heard a sound coming from down the road.

Billy looked and saw the truck that had passed them backing up.

"Well, look at that," he said, grinning.

The truck backed up to within five feet of the car, and stopped. The door of the cab opened and two men stepped out.

"Saw you going into it," said the driver, a young man about twenty. He knelt and looked under the car. "Transmission's touching. Hook up the chain, Ed. No way they'll get out of here without help."

The driver's co-worker hooked up a chain between the rear axles of the car and the truck, and in two minutes had the car back up on the road.

"Much thanks to you boys," said Mr. Chekko. "But — ah — you were coming down the road pretty fast, you know. I pulled way over because I was afraid —"

The driver smiled. "I'm not arguing with you, sir," he broke in pleasantly. "It was my fault. But don't worry. Our insurance will take care of the damages."

He took a pencil and small pad from his shirt pocket, scribbled something on the top sheet, tore it off and handed it to Billy's father. "That's my name, and the name of the insurance company. I'm sure they'll handle it for you. Sorry about what happened, but we've been on the go all day and would like to get done before sunset. Take care, now."

"You, too," said Mr. Chekko.

The men got back into the truck and drove off, speeding as fast as they had when Billy and his father had first encountered them coming down the road.

Mr. Chekko shook his head sadly. "A decent guy," he said, "otherwise he wouldn't have stopped. But look at him go. Know what that means, Billy? Now that we've got a car we've got to be on the alert more than ever. There are just too many careless drivers, nice guys or not, on the road."

They entered the car. "We might as well go home," decided Mr. Chekko, glancing at his wristwatch. "It's not six yet, but I don't feel right driving around with my front right fender and bumper banged in like they are." He looked at his son. "All right with you?"

"Sure, Dad."

Mr. Chekko started the car, checked to make certain the road was clear, and turned it around.

"Garages close at five," he said sadly as he headed back for home. "So I can't take the car to one till Saturday. Bull and horsefeathers. I guess I just don't live right."

"You and me both, Dad," said Billy. What a day

it had been. First the bet and the race, then Wendy's anger, now the car.

Since the car had to be repaired there was no telling when his father would get his driver's license. Billy'd have to keep doing his mother's errands on foot for at least another month, he thought despondently.

After a somber supper he waited patiently for Dan to finish reading the sports pages of the paper. Dan, it seemed, always finished eating before he did, and got to the paper first.

Christina seemed to find solace reading the comic page and Ann Landers until the sports pages were free for her to read at her leisure. At this time of day Sheri was giving her doll a bath and preparing her for bed, after which her own bedtime came.

Mr. Chekko, sitting in the living room with his ankles crossed and his fingertips pressed together, cleared his throat. "Billy," he said, "I've been thinking."

Billy looked at him gravely. "About cutting wood?"

His father laughed. "No, not about cutting wood. About that accident. I noticed you handled yourself pretty well."

Billy grinned. "Well, thanks, Dad." He could take

a compliment from his father anytime. "You did, too. I thought you'd get mad, but you didn't. You handled the whole thing quite nicely yourself."

Mr. Chekko shrugged. "Never mind that. What I want to say is, I'll teach you to drive."

Billy's eyes widened. He couldn't believe his ears. "You — you will?"

His father's eyes met his squarely. "That's what I said, didn't I?"

"Oh, wow! Thanks, Dad! Thanks a million! Hey, you're the greatest, you know that? Just the greatest, Dad!"

His excitement had reached a peak when he heard Dan's droll voice cut in, "Hey, Billy. Listen to this. Cove Hill's having a meet with Hamlin on Thursday," he read from the paper. "They've gone undefeated so far. Did you know that?"

"No. And don't tell me about it," said Billy, still bubbling with joy over the news his father had given him. Nothing could be better news than that!

Dan read on silently for a while, then cried out, his interest shown by the expression on his face, "Hey, Billy, here's more. 'Both the one-mile and two-mile races were won easily by Hamlin's Scott Nichols, a junior, who hasn't lost a race since he joined track in his freshman year. The tall, easy-going youth is the fastest long-distance runner this community has seen in a long time.' Fastest, baloney. I never heard of him. Have you?"

"That's because you haven't been reading about track till I got started in it," said Billy. "Yes, I've heard of him. And I guess he's good, from what I've read."

A grin spread across his brother's face. "Hey, man, wouldn't it be great if Coach Seavers had you run against him?"

"You want to see him make a fool of me, too?"

"No! I told you, Billy. I know you've run long distances, over hills and rocks and through weeds and everything. You'd be good in cross-country. But I bet you could beat anybody in the mile and two-mile. Anybody. Including this Scott Nichols."

Billy smiled, touched. "Know what? Every once in a while you surprise the hell out of me, Dan."

Dan frowned. "What d'you mean?"

"Well, you're sticking up for me. Even though I sometimes act like a second father to you, and you get sore at me, you still come back on my side when the chips are down."

"Heck, why shouldn't I?" Dan said. "We're brothers, aren't we?"

Chapter 14

THERE WAS track practice after school on Tuesday. Billy attended it. A callous on the back of his heel was the only sign left of the blister. And he had no worry of getting a fresh one; his new track shoes fit him perfectly.

If Coach Seavers saw him there — and there was no doubt in Billy's mind that he did — he didn't show it. Billy was among the runners near the track, stretching and hopping up and down to limber their muscles and condition their hearts for the vigorous runs ahead. The high jumpers, broad jumpers, pole vaulters, and discus throwers were in their respective sections, working under the guidance of Coach Rafini.

There weren't more than a dozen kids watching. They wore sweaters or jackets with their collars turned up. The sun hadn't shone all day, and a stiff breeze was sweeping across the field. Even Coach Seavers was wearing a jacket over his sweatshirt.

Billy tried to avoid getting too close to Cody, who was hopping up and down with Luke and Rudy, preparing for the sixty-yard sprint.

The sight of Cody only reminded him of the bet he had lost, and that Wendy probably would never speak to him again. He had looked for her today, but hadn't seen her. He wouldn't be surprised if she never came to another meet. And he couldn't blame her.

He noticed the absence of Pearl McCarthy and the skinny brunette, too. Either the weather was too cold for Pearl, or she had heard about the bet and it had made her angry with Cody.

Maybe Cody doesn't care beans for Pearl, but the dumb bet has certainly ended things between Wendy and me, Billy thought dismally.

"Okay, Cody," Coach Seavers piped up. "You, Rudy, and Seattle line up for the sixty-yard sprint." He then ordered one of the other runners standing by to wait for his command to start, gave him the gun, and walked rapidly down to the finish line.

"Okay, start!" he yelled.

"On your mark! Get set!" *Bang!* went the gun.

Cody was ahead almost immediately, and came in first easily, two steps ahead of Seattle. The one hundred, two-twenty, and four-forty followed in order, with ten-minute rest periods between each race. Cody ran in all of them, and took the one hundred and two-twenty again with no surprise to anyone.

Chuck Schwinn beat him out in the four-forty. Schwinn also won the one-hundred-eighty-yard hurdle by four lengths, and squeezed into first place by a step in the two-hundred-yard hurdle. Koski led all the way in the eight-eighty, winning it easily.

Two other runners competed with him in the hurdles, neither of whom seemed fast enough to put a scare into any school.

The mile race was next, and Billy waited anxiously for the coach to announce his name.

"Joy! Maynard! Koski! Line up for the mile! Hustle, you guys! It's getting late!" The coach clapped his hands hard as he called off the runners' names and yelled the order. Billy stood like a statue, refusing to believe that the coach wouldn't let him run. The coach asked another runner to give them the starting signal, then turned and headed toward the finish line behind him.

What's the matter with me? Billy wanted to yell at him. I'm okay! And I can run! I can!

Without thinking about it another second he ran to the starting line and entered the number four lane next to Dick Koski. He saw Koski glance at him, surprised, but didn't return his gaze.

The starter began calling, "On your mark! Get set!" *Bang!* went the gun.

They took off. After twenty yards Billy found himself four steps behind Koski, who had taken the lead. Soon Rudy moved ahead of him, arms and legs pumping hard. At the quarter-of-a-mile mark Rudy took the lead.

Billy maintained an even pace, not going any faster than he had when the race had started. But at the half-mile mark he picked up speed, and by the time he reached the three-quarters-of-a-mile mark he had overtaken Rudy and Koski. Rudy had fallen slightly behind again, trailing Koski by five yards.

Billy was in the lead now, and going strong. He was hardly tired. His legs felt fine.

When he came to the finish line, far ahead of Koski, he disregarded the surprised look the coach gave him. He ran on for twenty more yards or so down the track, slowing his pace down to nothing. Then he ran off to the side and rested.

He expected the coach to yell at him, to chew him out for running when he wasn't asked to; or else to shower praise on him for beating the others. But the coach only glanced at him and said nothing.

Is Coach Seavers ignoring me on purpose? Billy wondered. Is he conserving his anger to hurl at me later?

Fifteen minutes later Koski and Maynard were called to the starting line for the two-mile race. There was a pause. Then Billy heard the coach call his name. "Chekko! Get in there!"

Billy grinned, and ran onto the track and got in the number three lane next to Koski.

The starter called the signals, fired the gun, and the runners took off. Maynard grabbed the lead and held it for half a mile. Koski kept a position almost side by side with Billy. It was all that Billy could do to keep from smiling. He knew what Dick's strategy was. He'd keep even with Billy, then take off when Billy did, and toward the end of the race he'd fly off all by himself to the finish line.

But it didn't work out that way, as Billy knew it wouldn't.

He was even with Maynard at the end of the first mile, then got into the lead and kept spreading the gap with almost every stride after that. Both Koski and Maynard made a last sprinting effort to catch up to him, but he let them come on, knowing that the effort would only take more energy out of them.

They fell back quickly, and he finished forty yards ahead of Koski, sixty ahead of Maynard.

He didn't stop when it was over, but continued to run toward the school.

"Chekko!" he heard the coach's voice yelling behind him.

Billy slowed to a stop, and turned around.

"See you Thursday!" said the coach.

"Yes, sir!" answered Billy.

He ran on to the school, showered, got dressed, and then ran all the way home.

The next morning he saw Wendy in the hall, walking with Pearl, and instantly he decided that he must talk to her. He had to do something to mend their torn friendship.

He started to run and caught up to her just before she turned into a classroom. "Wendy!" he called.

She stared over her shoulder at him, shot him a glazed look, and went on into the room. He followed her in, aware that there were already a dozen kids inside.

"Wendy, I've got to talk to you," he insisted. "You've got to hear me out. Give me a minute, will you? Thirty seconds?"

She sat down, plopped a book on her desk, and flipped it open. Billy, feeling a dozen pairs of eyes centering on him, blushed with embarrassment and headed for his own desk.

Another round lost, he thought, as his spirits sank another notch.

Chapter 15

BILLY RODE the bus home after school, taking his duffel bag with him. Without wasting any time, he put on his trunks and shoes and ran to Ulster Road, up to the highway and south on it to Jay's Soft Ice Cream Shop. The full distance was about five miles. He considered buying a soft ice cream cone to satisfy the thirst he had developed, but resisted the temptation and ran all the way back, sprinting the short distance home from Ulster Road. He still had time to shower before supper.

The big news at the supper table was his.

"I'm running in the mile and two-mile in Thursday's meet against Hamlin," he said happily, not afraid to show his excitement. "How about that? I think that the coach is finally convinced I can run."

"What about your sore heel?" asked Dan, grabbing up a forkful of baked potato from his plate.

"It's healed up fine. Anyway, it wasn't only because of my heel that the coach didn't ask me to run. He didn't think I could compete."

Dan smiled. "I guess it was a good thing you got on the track and proved yourself, showed that you could run," he said. "Otherwise you'd probably still be on the sideline."

"Right," said Billy.

"Well, the coach has got a job to do," said Billy's father. "He's there to develop a bunch of kids into good runners, jumpers, or whatever a kid wants to do. He's also a father figure, a man who believes in discipline, but wants to make sure his kids don't take unnecessary risks. He might've thought he was doing the right thing in not letting you run, Billy. Maybe you proved to him that he could be wrong once in a while."

"I hope so," smiled Billy.

The day of the meet against Hamlin High was typical for May. Clouds scudded across the sky, shielding the sun part of the time as a warm breeze kept moving them westward. The crowd attending was larger than usual, probably because word had gotten around that Cove Hill was meeting Hamlin, the only undefeated team in the league.

Billy watched the sixty-yard dash captured by a Hamlin sophomore, who won it by a step over Cody Jones.

The loss drew a moan from the Cove Hill fans. It was the first time they had seen their sprint idol lose the sixty-yarder.

"Beans," said Rudy, standing near Billy's right elbow. "If Cody lost that one, he'll probably lose the hundred, too."

"The kid got a head start on him," said Luke. "He won't do it again, I betcha."

He was right. Cody won the one-hundred by a step and a half.

"What'd I tell you?" said Luke, grinning.

Billy saw some people coming up on his left side. Turning, he saw that it was Pearl McCarthy and her satellite, the skinny, dark-haired girl. And — he looked again to make sure — Wendy Thaler was there, too.

"Hi, Billy," Pearl greeted him.

"Hi, Pearl," he said.

"Hi," said the girl next to her.

"Hi," said Billy.

Wendy said nothing. Her attention seemed to be riveted on the track where hardly anything was going on at the moment.

She's ignoring me, thought Billy. So what else is new?

He didn't speak to her, either. He wanted to. He wanted to desperately. But why waste his breath if all she might do was answer him with a cold stare?

The one-hundred-eighty-yard hurdle was next. A tall, high-jumping youth for Hamlin won it by half a dozen steps. Cove Hill came in second, and the second Hamlin runner third. Each school was represented by two runners.

"We've got to do something," urged Rudy, prancing around like a nervous colt. "A kid just came from the high jumps and said that Ham won that, too."

Scores were rated on the place won by a competitor. First place was rated five, second place three, third place one. Unless Cove Hill scored enough first place wins Hamlin would go home undefeated again.

Billy saw Coach Seavers talking with Vice Principal Keating and two teachers. He was standing with his hands clasped behind him, nervously scrubbing the palm of one hand with the fist of the other. There was no doubt how he was feeling about the results of the races so far. He had been sure that Cody would take the shorter races, but Cody had already lost the sixty-yarder. The second place finish in the one-hundred-eighty-yard hurdles was hardly enough to build up any confidence.

The two-hundred-twenty-yard dash came up. Yale and Mackey represented Hamlin, Seattle and Cody, Cove Hill.

Right from the sound of the starting shot Yale

took the lead. Seattle and Cody passed him and ran neck and neck. Near the fifty-yard mark Yale crept up and surged ahead. Gradually Seattle left Cody behind him and closed the gap between himself and Yale. Both runners puffed hard as they swiftly approached the finish line. There was a roar from the fans of both Cove Hill and Hamlin as the two runners crossed it, Yale the winner by a step.

"Seattle waited too long for that final fast sprint," Rudy said, disgruntled. "He could've beaten the kid."

Maybe, thought Billy. But maybe the Hamlin runner would have started his final sprint earlier, too.

A hand grabbed his left arm. "Chekko."

Billy turned, surprised, and saw that it was Coach Seavers.

"How would you like to run in the eight-eighty?"

"Sure."

"Okay. Be ready for it. Rudy's running with you. The four-forty is next, and I'm having Schwinn and Cody run it. I'm looking for Schwinn to take it. How you feeling?"

"Okay."

The coach guessed right. Schwinn won the four-forty by half a dozen steps. Cody came in third.

Hamlin won first place in the medley relay. Cove

Hill came in second and third. Word came that Colloni had won the discus-throwing event. The points were piling up.

The eight-eighty was ready to start.

The gunshot. The start. Rudy took the lead and held it for a third of the distance, Billy trailing behind him by five steps. Hamlin crept up and took the lead and Billy stepped up his pace. He ran smoothly, a liquid, graceful rhythm to his long, easy strides. He kept his knees high, landing on the balls of his feet, then pushing himself forward for the next step.

He thought of nothing except the run. Concentration was the all-important thing now. Everything else was of no consequence.

He was third at the halfway marker, still third at the six-sixty. Rudy was second, a Hamlin runner first.

With about sixty yards yet to go, Billy felt it was time to put on steam. Just as if he had garnered a fresh supply of energy, he flew ahead, racing past Rudy and then the Hamlin runner, who came in second four yards behind him.

From the Cove Hill fans came a roar that was the loudest Billy had heard in a long time. He was congratulated from all directions, patted on the back, praised. He was stunned. He couldn't believe it himself.

Even Pearl and her skinny friend offered their congratulations. Where is Wendy? he asked himself. He looked for her, and finally saw her standing alone just beyond the girls.

He went over to her. "Wendy," he said, "will you listen to me a minute? I don't care if you never speak to me again. But I've got to tell you this. I'm sorry about that stupid bet."

A voice interrupted him. "Chekko! Come here!"

He turned, saw the coach waving to him, and ran off.

"Yes, Coach?"

"I want to see your heel," said the coach.

"My heel? Why? It's okay. It's been okay."

"Sit down. Take off your shoe. I want to see it, Chekko."

Tightening his lips, Billy sat down, took off the shoe and the sock. The coach bent down, grabbed the foot and twisted it to get a good look at the heel.

A smile came to his face, disappeared as quickly. "Good," he said, dropping the foot. "I had to be sure, Chekko. Come on. I want to talk to you, Rudy, and Luke about the mile and the two-mile runs. We've got to win them, Chekko. Somehow we've got to pull this thing off."

* * *

Running the one-mile race were Billy and Rudy for Cove Hill, Scott Nichols and Tom Waters for Hamlin.

From the shot of the gun Waters took the lead and kept it most of the way, with Nichols trailing behind him about five yards. Billy remained behind Nichols for half a mile, then slowly moved ahead. Nichols, too, increased his pace, but Billy kept moving up closer and closer to him.

Near the three-quarter-mile mark Waters fell behind, overtaken by Nichols and Billy. As they entered the final quarter Nichols was in the lead by ten yards. Billy was second.

Now Billy put on his drive and began to fly. There were still twenty yards to go when he exerted all the power in his legs and sailed by Nichols. He kept putting distance between him and the Hamlin runner, and crossed the finish line by five yards.

Again the congratulations, the handshakes, the many praises.

"Nice running, Chekko," said Coach Seavers with admiration. "Take the two-mile, and I'll see that you'll have your picture in the paper."

The two-mile race, thought Billy, shouldn't be any more difficult than the one-mile. He felt that, because he had beaten Nichols in the shorter distance, he should win easily in the longer.

But it wasn't so.

Waters again took an early lead. Nichols was second, Billy third, Rudy last.

Suddenly Nichols started to sprint, and continued to for about fifty yards, leaving the remaining three runners trailing far behind him.

Billy thought he recognized the strategy in the move. Nichols wanted to maintain a good lead, then reserve his energy while running at a slower pace. After they had run about a quarter of a mile Nichols might repeat the strategy, and grab a lead that might make it impossible for anyone to catch up to him.

But, before Billy would let this happen, he picked up speed and came up to within a yard of Nichols before he settled down to an even, relaxed stride.

For a while he watched Nichols, and saw the tall youth land low on the ball of each foot, drop to his heel, then drive forward from his toes. It was the same technique that Billy had been taught. But there was more to running than that. A runner had to know how to distribute his energy evenly over the distance he had to cover. Billy was reasonably sure he had developed this knowledge. The runs he had made between his home and the grocery store and drugstore in New Court had built up the muscles in his legs and conditioned his lungs long before he had joined the track team. Joining the team had mainly cultivated his style of running, made him aware of various running speeds and different lengths of stride, and when to use them. Scott Nichols was probably aware of these facts as well.

It was at the three-quarters-of-a-mile mark that Nichols sprinted for about fifty yards, pulling himself far ahead of Billy. The other two runners had increased their speed, too, but were still trailing, Rudy by about ten yards, the Hamlin runner by fifteen.

Billy increased his speed, but not into a sprint. He felt that as long as he kept within ten yards or so of Nichols, at least for the first mile, Nichols wouldn't pose a threat. And by running at a fast, even pace he could reserve his energy for the time that he would really need it.

They passed the mile mark, and Billy saw the gap widening again between himself and Nichols.

He felt he was forced now into running faster, too. He couldn't let Nichols get too far ahead of him in order to be able to sail smoothly to the finish line. He sprinted for about sixty yards, then settled down again to a comfortable, relaxed stride.

With half a mile yet to go Billy could see that he was gaining on Nichols, who was now about seven or eight yards ahead of him. With a quarter of a mile left they were even, and Nichols began to sprint. Billy let him go. Nichols sprinted for about fifty yards, then slowed down. Billy could see he was beat.

They were neck and neck, with about fifty yards to go to the finish line, when Billy passed him. With twenty yards yet to go, Billy heard Nichols coming up fast behind him.

Then, out of the corner of his eye, Billy saw Nichols beside him.

Oh, no, you won't! he thought, and galvanized his legs into a sprint that carried him forward like a catapult. In just a few strides he crossed the finish line, five yards ahead of Nichols.

Billy didn't know till later that Rudy had come in third. But now he didn't care. He had won the two-mile race, running it the fastest he had run in his life.

He was suddenly surrounded by fans who cheered and applauded him. A photographer from the *Lonsdale Tribune* took pictures of him and the other winners.

"You came through like a champ, Chekko," exclaimed Coach Seavers, gripping his hand. "For the first time in years, we're number one."

Billy smiled, took a towel that someone had thrust into his hands, and wiped his face.

"Billy?"

He looked around at the owner of the familiar voice. "Hi, Wendy," he whispered.

"Congratulations," she said. She was smiling. She looked beautiful.

"Thanks. Hey, can — can I talk to you?"

"About what?"

"The movie on Saturday."

"Why? Can't you go?" The wind was teasing her hair.

"Oh, sure, I can. But that bet. I wanted to tell you it wasn't my idea."

"I know. And it makes no difference. I told Cody I wouldn't go with him if he were the last creature on earth."

"You did?"

"Yes, I did."

He grabbed her hand. He was suddenly cool and relaxed. He felt so good.

"Will you walk with me down to the school?" he asked.

She squeezed his hand. "Come on," she said.